HEIRS
OF HOLLOWDALE HIGH

HEIRS
OF HOLLOWDALE HIGH

KATIE LOWRIE

contents

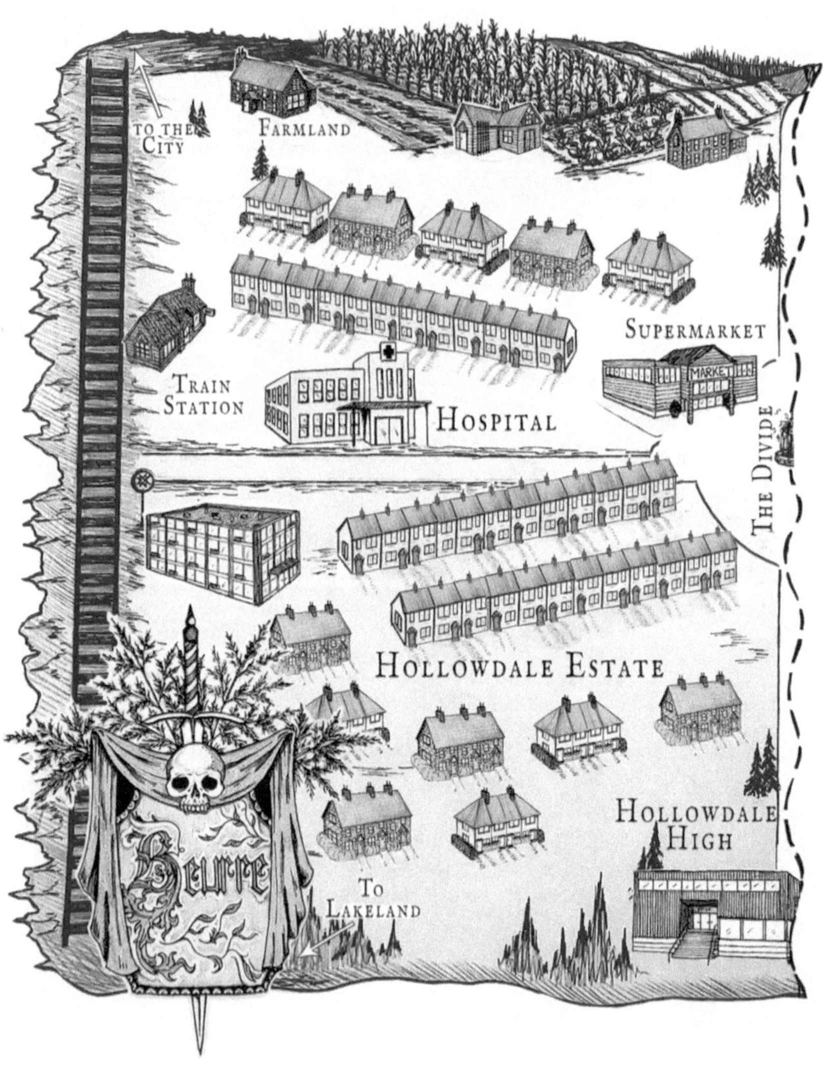

TO THE CITY
FARMLAND
SUPERMARKET
MARKET
TRAIN STATION
HOSPITAL
THE DIVIDE
HOLLOWDALE ESTATE
HOLLOWDALE HIGH
Beurre
To LAKELAND

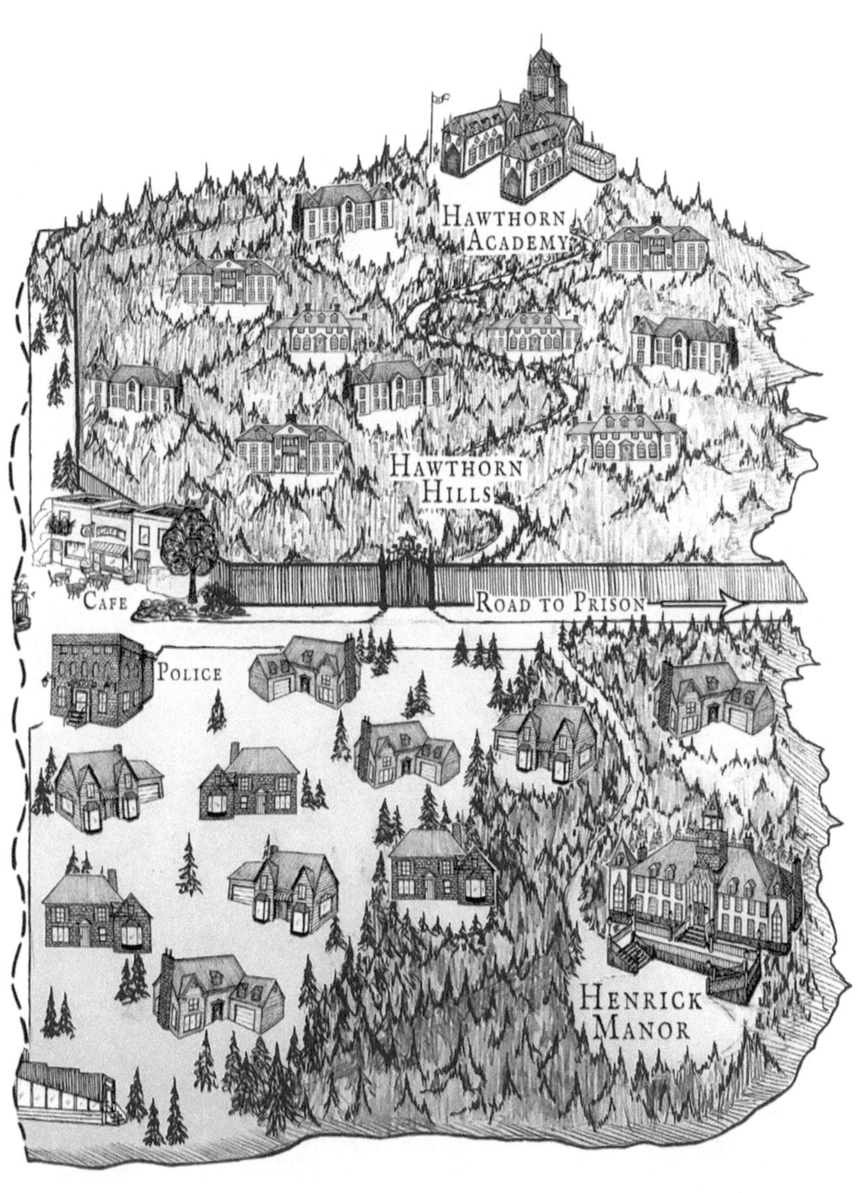

Hawthorn Academy
Hawthorn Hills
Cafe
Road to Prison
Police
Henrick Manor

To the things kept out of reach

author's note

Thank you so much for picking up a copy of *Heirs of Hollowdale High*.

It's about time Arianna and Rock were given the chance to tell their story.

This story deals with some real life themes and issues that could be potential triggers.
You can head to my website for any trigger/content warnings you may need.

Enjoy!

Arianna

age 14, july

THE SUN SHONE from the moment I woke up.

Even the sun thought the day was going to be a good one. Which was a fucking joke, really. A joke the universe was playing on me—and only me.

'You look beautiful.'

I pulled myself from my thoughts and looked at Gigi, smiling through my inner turmoil. She made a beautiful bride. Of course she did. My dad wouldn't be marrying her if she wasn't beautiful. He was a typical wealthy dickhead with more money than sense, and he was on his third wife already. And I hadn't ruled out that he would one day have a fourth.

My mum died when I was a baby, meaning I could barely remember much about her, and all I had was a couple of photographs to keep me going. Dad married again not long after, I supposed he didn't want to be a single father for long, even though she never felt like a mum to me, but they divorced a couple of years ago after a lengthy battle for my father's wealth. A battle in which he won. Nobody gets the best of Tony Hollowdale.

Then about six months ago, he bumped into Gigi at a local

restaurant and sparks flew. Or some bullshit like that. Every time she told the story, a little bit of sick made its way into my mouth and I had to excuse myself pretty sharpish. Otherwise, I'd have blown chunks all over the people present.

And in no time at all, here we all were at their wedding.

While I was in my own personal hell.

Because the guy I'd had a crush on forever was going to be my new stepbrother.

'WELL, don't you scrub up nice!'

Gray walked towards me, a drink in his hand, a wry smile on his face, and all I wanted to do was deck him one. Who did he think he was, swaggering over to me with that expression? Didn't he know I was in hell just waiting for the devil to come over and show me to my cage for all eternity?

'Shame about you, isn't it?' I said back, assessing him from head to toe with a narrowed gaze. His hair was brushed back and styled, neater than usual, and his blue eyes were filled with joy. He was wearing a suit a couple of sizes too big for him, and I knew he'd be wearing it to the funeral next month, too. Instantly, you could tell it was his father's suit, not just because it was big on him, but also because I knew they didn't have the money for him to get a new one. Not that it mattered. I only got a new dress for the cursed day because I was a bridesmaid and it was expected of me. My dad told me in no uncertain terms that I wasn't to give Gigi any grief. Anything she wanted was to be hers, no ands, ifs, or buts about it.

'I look a pretty picture. I'll have you know.'

'Who says?'

'Your new *stepmother*,' he said, a glint of menace in his eyes.

He knew how much I hated thinking about Gigi as my stepmother. 'First thing she said when she saw me.'

'Yeah, yeah. We all know she's got a soft spot for you.'

'She's always liked you, too,' he pointed out, still beaming at me, getting a kick out of the entire thing. 'She just happens to like your dad better.'

'Makes me wonder if she likes my dad or his money.'

'Stop being such a cynic, Ree. They're in love. You can see it from her new designer bags and that new car she's been seen driving around Beurre.'

We both broke out into laughter, hidden away at the side of the dance floor.

'What are you two laughing at?' Tyler asked, followed by Rock and Ace. The three of them each had a drink in their hands and were dressed in their best suits. They all looked really handsome, but only one of them caught my eye, and of course it was the one I shouldn't be looking at.

'How well you've scrubbed up,' Gray joked, pushing Tyler's shoulder. 'Who's ready to dance the night away?'

'Not me,' Ace answered, his eyes fixed on a girl across the room. A cousin of Rock's or something. 'I plan to get to know *her* a little better.'

'Leave my family alone,' Rock replied, a threat in his voice. 'Last thing any of them need is you coming onto them.'

'I'll have you know, *Andrew,* that I'm a very charming young man.'

'And who told you that?' Rock seethed, pissed that Ace dared to call him a name that wasn't even his real name. His actual name was Drew, but nobody used it. Ace just called him Andrew to irritate him on purpose. I never thought of him as Drew, though, and it was super bloody weird to think of him as anything other than Rock.

He'd always be Rock to me.

'Your mum,' Ace said, a cheeky grin on his face. A peek of his tongue darted out to lick his bottom lip.

'Your mum's been giving out all the compliments today, to be fair,' Gray said. 'She told me I look a pretty picture earlier.'

'Well, my mum's on cloud nine, ain't she?' Rock looked over at where his mum was talking to her maid of honour, a wide, beaming smile covering her face, and I couldn't help but notice how happy she looked. Even if she was with my dad for money, she seemed genuinely happy about it all.

'And is your dad on cloud nine, Ari?' Ace asked, nudging me in the side.

'Not a clue,' I replied, moving my gaze to my dad. Tony Hollowdale was standing in a group, telling some amusing story, no doubt, in order to charm those around him. He always did that. Charmed everybody with a smile or a quick-witted response. It was a shame he couldn't treat his own daughter with the same respect and civility he gave complete strangers. 'He's definitely spent enough money on today.'

'You saying my mum isn't worth it?' Rock asked, his piercing gaze cutting me to the core, but then his lips turned up into a soft smile and I breathed a small sigh of relief that he was messing with me.

'Well, my inheritance is definitely going to be a lot less after today. I might not even be a millionaire when dear Papa dies.'

'Aw, now that would be a shame, wouldn't it? What a spoiled little rich girl,' Gray teased. 'Your privilege is showing, Ree.'

I shoved him in the side and rolled my eyes at him. The boy was doing all he could to push my buttons—and it was working. Like he didn't know how on edge I was already.

The music stopped, and the DJ came over the speakers.

'It gives me great pleasure to welcome to the dance floor, Mr and Mrs Hollowdale!'

The room erupted with loud cheers, hoots, and the clinking of glasses. My dad left the group he was standing with and moved over to his new bride, taking her hand in his and sweeping her onto the dance floor.

They both looked at each other, happier than I'd ever seen them, and I swallowed my discomfort at the entire situation.

If my dad was happy—truly happy—then I had to accept my fate. Had to accept that I could never act on my feelings for Rock. Simple as.

No matter how much that thought depressed me.

One

Arianna

age 17, july

THE START of another summer holiday.

The start of another torturous six weeks of being at home with Rock and no parents around.

Like they'd done ever since they got married, the two of them headed off to the Bahamas the moment the two of us finished school for the year, with a quick wave goodbye and a 'Have fun!' called behind them as they went.

You would think that after our parents being married for nearly four years, the two of us would be adjusted to the fact we were stepsiblings and therefore off-limits—but nope. If anything, things were even more frosty between us now than they'd ever been.

Our relationship was non-existent. Our friendship was even worse.

We could barely stand in the same room as each other without biting each other's heads off. Every little thing Rock did irritated me these days, and I hated that it did, but I couldn't help it. It was easier to be irritated by him than to lust over him after all.

Then there was the fact that in the last year he'd got himself a girlfriend.

Savannah Rhodes was her name, and fuck, I couldn't stand her.

Was it because she was Rock's girlfriend? Maybe.

Was I judging her harshly? Probably.

Did I give a fuck? Meh. It depended on the day.

Savannah was pretty, blonde, and completely vapid. I didn't want to believe *that* was Rock's type, but clearly, he liked her as they were nearing their year anniversary.

'Why do you have such a sour face?'

'What?' I snapped, turning to face Rock, who had snuck up on me while I stared into the distance, my eyes having landed on the bird feeder and the squirrel that was nibbling from it.

'Why do you look like somebody pissed in your Cornflakes?'

I rolled my eyes. *What a charmer.*

'I didn't realise I looked like that, but thanks for the heads-up. I'll make sure to rearrange my features when Tyler stops by.'

'Tyler's coming over?'

'Yep,' I said with conviction, even though Tyler had absolutely no plans to pop over, and I needed to somehow get away from Rock and send him a message ASAP so that he would. 'Think we're going to see a movie.'

'What movie?' he asked, narrowing his eyes on my telltale flush.

'Err...' *Shit. Why couldn't I remember any film that was out?* 'That new one with that actor.'

'What actor?'

'Oh, you know the one...' I trailed off, hoping Rock would supply me with some kind of something that I could take and run away with. 'Was in that big blockbuster last summer.'

'Oh, him,' Rock said with a nod. 'Sure. Sounds like you're going to have fun.'

'I always have fun with Tyler.' I smiled, knowing that Tyler was a sore spot for Rock, but using him to tease him anyway. I pulled my phone out of my pocket and looked at it as if whatever I was looking at didn't hold much importance, as I touched on to my conversation with Tyler.

> Hey, I need you to come take me to the cinema. No questions asked. You owe me.

I just hoped he remembered what he owed me for…

> Told Rock I was stopping by?

Even though the words were just letters on my phone, I could see the expression Tyler was giving me through them, and I knew he could see my bullshit from a mile away.

> Just get here. And soon. Okay?

> Be with you in ten.

> Thank you! I owe you one

> Damn straight.

'Is that Tyler?' Rock asked, nudging his head to the phone I was gripping so tight in my palm that my knuckles were turning white.

'Yeah. He's going to be here in ten.'

'I'll stick around to see him, then.'

'Why? Don't you have somewhere you need to be?'

'Like?'

'Out with your *girlfriend*, perhaps?'

'If I didn't know any better, Ari, I'd say you sounded jealous.'

'Jealous?' I spat. 'Of *what* exactly?'

'Of Savannah.'

'Why would I be jealous of her of all people?'

'All I'm saying, Ari, is that your green-eyed monster is showing.'

'And all *I'm* saying, Rock, is that your dickheaded true self is showing.'

'Whatever you say, *princess.*'

The nickname was mocking and whenever he used it, he didn't mean it in a nice way. It was the name Tyler called me, and one Rock took the piss out of as much as he could whenever the chance struck.

He took a step closer to me, and I took a step back, not wanting the distance between us to close.

Needing that distance to keep myself afloat and away from him.

Because, to me, his pecs were a magnet, drawing me closer and closer until I couldn't get away without harming myself in the process.

But he didn't give a fuck about my retreat because he took yet another step closer.

'You scared, Ari?'

'Scared of what?' I stuttered, my bottom lip all aquiver, giving my true thoughts away.

'Scared of what you feel for me.'

'Who said I feel anything for you but disdain?'

'Keep telling yourself that.'

Another step.

And another.

Until my back was up against the wall, quite literally, and he was a mere inch away from me, his face so close that his breath skittered across my skin, and I shivered at the nearness of him. *Fuck me.*

'You'd like that, wouldn't you?'

Shit. Balls. Fuck.

'Did I say that out loud?' I whispered, mortified that my inner thoughts had left my lips and entered the air around us.

'You did.'

'Oh.'

'Ari, I—'

'No!' I cut him off, not wanting to hear what he had to say about it. 'No, let's not.'

'Ari, please.'

'Step away, Rock,' I said, my tone filled with pleading. 'I won't ask again.'

He took a step back with an almost imperceptible nod, knowing when to stop pushing me.

I opened my mouth to say something more, but the doorbell rang, and I used it as my excuse to get out of the tense situation I'd somehow found myself in.

On quick feet, I rushed to the door, so excited to see Tyler's face on the other side, but it wasn't Tyler waiting there when I opened it.

No.

It was Savannah Rhodes. Looking like an angel, with the smile of a demon.

'Oh, Savannah. It's you.'

'It's me,' she tittered. 'Why? Were you expecting me to be somebody else?'

'Tyler's on his way,' I replied, opening the door wider for her to enter, hoping Rock would appear behind me and save me from her presence, but he didn't. Wanker was probably holding back on purpose. 'Rock!'

'Oh, hey, babe,' he said, entering the hall. 'I didn't hear the door go.'

Fucking liar.

'That's okay.' She walked into his open arms for a tight hug, burrowing her head in his chest, while I stood like a lemon and watched. 'Arianna was her charming self as usual.'

'She's a known charmer,' Rock said, winking at me over the top of Savannah's head. 'Everybody says it.'

'Whatever.' As I pushed the door to close it, Tyler appeared and I breathed a deep sigh of relief. His warm blue eyes had always filled me with a happiness I couldn't quite explain. My friendship with Tyler was different to the one I had with Grayson but just as important.

Grayson was the person I would die beside. The boy who always had my back and would never ever judge me for any of my actions. For any of my mistakes.

Tyler was my closest friend that wasn't Gray. We were friends, but not so close that we'd open up about everything going on in our lives, but we still knew enough about each other to form a tight unit.

'Hey, princess,' he said, leaning down and placing a kiss on my hair. 'You ready to go?'

'You bet!' I said, drumming up enthusiasm I didn't completely feel. *Fake it until you make it and all that shit.*

'What film are you going to see?' Rock piped up, a mischievous glint in his eye. 'I already asked Ari, but she couldn't tell me. Just said it had an actor in it that was in a film last year.'

He laughed, and Tyler laughed too, but the tension in the room was high.

It was as if everybody was talking about one thing but thinking another.

We need to get the fuck out of here.

'Well, as fun as this is,' I said, grabbing Tyler's arm and gripping him close, 'we've got to head out if we want to be on time.'

Nobody mentioned that we still hadn't named the film we were rushing to go see.

'Nice to see you, Savannah,' Tyler said with a wide smile, then he turned to Rock and nodded. 'Rock.'

'See you later,' I said, practically dragging Tyler out the door. 'Don't wait up!'

'It's midday,' Rock deadpanned.

'Oh, shut up!' I shouted and stomped to Tyler's car, pissed at myself, and mostly pissed at the fact I was letting him get to me in the first place.

'You're playing it really cool, princess,' Tyler whispered in my ear and a snort left me unbidden. 'You're the epitome of calm.'

'Just get me out of here.'

'Your wish is my command, princess.'

TWO
ROCK

age 17, july

'THE TWO OF them make a cute couple, don't they?' Savannah took a bite of her apple, her eyes transfixed on the TV in my room, lost in thought.

'Who do?' The sound of her crunching the apple wormed its way into my ears and it made me squirm. There was something about the way Savannah ate an apple that bothered me, amongst other things she did, and I wondered sometimes if I found fault with her because I wasn't that into her.

But then I'd shake it off.

Savannah was a great girl, and the two of us had a great relationship, but sometimes I wondered if there was more out there.

'Arianna and Tyler, of course.'

Huh? My head snapped to face her.

'They're not a couple.' The words were a rush. Certain. Adamant. 'They're just good friends.'

'Good friends?' Sav laughed. 'The two of them spend just as much time together as we do.'

'That's not true.' I shook my head and picked up the TV remote to turn down the volume, needing to do something with my hands. 'She spends more time with Gray.'

'Yeah, but it's obvious to anyone who knows them that she and Gray are just friends.'

'She's *just friends* with both of them. Ari isn't into anyone.'

'What makes you so sure about that? The two of you can barely stand each other.'

'That's not true.'

'Isn't it?' She threw her apple core in the wastepaper bin and turned to face me. 'Whenever I'm around, all you do is argue.'

'I suppose,' I conceded, not wanting to argue with her. 'Isn't that what happens with siblings, though? They get under each other's skin like no others can.'

'That's true. My sister pisses me off in a way nobody else does. Sometimes all she has to do is walk into a room and the air sours, along with my mood.'

'So, you get it.'

'Of course! But I also know when my sister's interested in somebody, and I would put money on Tyler and Ari liking one another.'

'Maybe you're right.' I leaned back against the headboard and she followed, throwing her leg over my side and placing her head on my chest. 'Maybe I'll ask Tyler at the field or something.'

'I could always ask Ari.'

'You think she'd tell you?'

Sav half shrugged against me. 'Probably not, but it wouldn't hurt to ask, would it?'

'Ari's a pretty private person. Doesn't really like opening up to people—especially people she isn't close with.'

'Ah, but a drink works wonders on a person's tongue. We can ambush them at the field. You talk to Tyler and I'll talk to Ari.'

'Sure,' I said, wanting her to stop the line of conversation and move on to something else. Something that didn't make my blood boil and my skin feel itchy.

The room began to feel too hot, but I couldn't move out from underneath Sav without her questioning me.

'I really do want to be her friend, you know?'

'Why?' I blurted, then calmed my tone. 'I mean, why do you need to be friends with her?'

'If we're going to be together for a long time,' she said, nudging me in the ribs, 'then I should be friends with your sister, shouldn't I?'

'She's not my sister,' I grumbled, contradicting my earlier point about siblings getting under one another's skin, and not giving a fuck about it.

'She's as good as.'

Wonderful. Just what I've always wanted.

Three

Arianna

age 17, august

'DID you and Tyler have a good time at the cinema?'

'Huh?' My head whipped in the direction of Savannah from where I'd been transfixed looking at Tyler and Rock across the field, and I rearranged the frown on my face fast but felt pretty certain she saw it anyway. It was a week after Tyler and I had gone to the cinema, and I'd forgotten about it mostly. We'd seen a movie that wasn't the best, but it kept up the ruse I'd built for us.

'You and Tyler,' Savannah said as if I was too simple to understand her. 'Did you enjoy your *date*?'

'It wasn't a date!' *And why on earth would she think it was?*

'No need to be coy with me.' Her voice was sweet like syrup but sticky enough that I needed to make sure I didn't get caught up in her web. 'I've seen the way you two look at each other.'

'You have?' I asked, dumbfounded for two reasons. One, that she was talking to me in the first place without anybody else around—at the field of all places. And two, that she was clearly seeing something nobody else did, because Tyler and I didn't look at each other in any sort of way other than one of friend-ship. My eyebrows were climbing higher on my face, the disbe-lief pouring out of me in waves.

Savannah nodded, taking a dainty sip from her straw, the contents in her cup looking as sickly sweet as her tone. A mix of orange and red—probably a sex on the beach knowing her.

'Well...' she continued, sly and slithering, 'it's either that, or you're looking at my boyfriend like that. Your own brother. What would people say about that?'

'How much have you had to drink?'

'Enough,' she answered and laughed, throwing her head back, the wind blowing through her long blonde hair that she'd straightened to shit. 'But even sober I can see how much you slobber over him. It's disgusting, really.'

It was my turn to laugh.

'Slobber? Me?' I shook my head. 'Okay, love.'

'You can laugh and deny all you want, *love*. I can see what's in your heart, and it's my boyfriend, so you better back the fuck off.'

'I barely talk to him, and when I do, it usually results in an argument.'

'So even you won't deny the chemistry that sizzles between you?'

'What the actual fuck?'

'Look, Arianna,' she said, prodding her pointy finger into my collarbone. 'I won't tell you again. You leave him alone and go slobber over somebody who actually *wants* you.'

'What is it with you and the word slobber?'

'Eurgh!' she growled, stamping her wedged heel on the dry grass. 'Why are you making this so difficult?'

'You two okay?'

Tyler's voice was like music to my ears. A balm to the soul. A —okay, you get the picture.

'Of course!' Savannah tittered, throwing her arm around me and pulling me close to her side, a little of her drink splashing my white top and no doubt staining it. 'Me and *princess* here were just having girl talk, isn't that right, Ree?'

'We sure were.' I put my arm around her and placed my

hand on her waist, pinching her enough that she loosened her grip on me.

Surely Tyler could see that my grin was bordering on demonic and I didn't mean any of it? That my tone was sarcastic as fuck? That the words came out through gritted teeth?

'If anybody's allowed to call Arianna princess, it's me,' he said with a laugh, reaching out to pull me into his side and away from the girl I didn't want to stand any closer to. 'She doesn't take kindly to strangers using it. Or calling her Ree, either.'

'You're so funny, Tyler!' Savannah cackled, touching his forearm as if she had the right. 'I'm not a stranger, silly.'

'Coulda fooled me,' I muttered.

The cool summer breeze whistled through the trees surrounding one edge of the field, and I paused to take it all in.

I had a love/hate relationship with summer, but there was one thing I couldn't deny, and that was how much I loved being outside on a summer evening.

Spencer's laughter travelled to where we were standing, and I looked over to see him chatting up a storm with a girl I didn't recognise.

Good for him.

Ace was beside them, a faint hint of amusement on his features, and I wondered if he'd potentially set them up and was giving himself a pat on the back—most likely prematurely.

I hadn't seen Gray since we'd arrived. No doubt he was off entertaining himself somehow or—should I say—with someone. Not like I should be surprised or anything. The boy was a nightmare, but he was my nightmare, and I wouldn't want him any other way.

'… a friendly warning, if you were.'

'A friendly what?' I asked, butting in, not having listened to a word that Sav and Tyler had said.

'Warning, apparently,' Tyler said, turning my face to his. 'Savannah here was giving us a friendly warning.'

'Is there such a thing?'

'Funny enough, no. I don't think there is.'

'That's what I thought, too.'

'Are you two even taking this seriously?' Sav snapped, annoyed we were talking as if she wasn't still there.

'This?' I asked, looking her up and down, taking in her too-tight vest top and denim skirt with a blink. 'Or *you*?'

She stomped her foot with a huff and turned away from us before flouncing off towards where Rock had joined Ace, Spencer, and the girl.

'She's a charmer.' Tyler chuckled and I smiled at him.

'Thanks for that.'

'For what?'

'For saving me from Sucky Savannah. I appreciate it.'

'Well, I appreciate you,' he said, moving to place his hands on each side of my hips. 'Do you think a kiss will really drive it home?'

'Drive what home?' My words were barely above a whisper, but Tyler had leaned down and he could hear each one.

'That you don't need her "friendly warning". That you give zero shits about her and Rock.'

'Us kissing didn't exactly work the way we wanted last time.'

A brief glance around told me that nobody was watching us —that I could see at least.

'Indulge me.' His whisper was a low seduction. A tease.

So, I took the plunge, went up on my tiptoes, and kissed him.

Four

Arianna

age 15, august

'Eurgh,' I said, the noise coming from the back of my throat. 'Look at him over there. Thinking he's some kind of shitty Casanova.'

'Just ignore him, princess.' Tyler's tone was one of boredom. He'd listened to me bitch about Rock on more than one occasion over the years and I knew it grated on him anytime I did it, but I couldn't stop. It was like a compulsion. My tongue ran off before my mind caught up with it, and by the time my mind caught up, it was too late to stop the train.

'It's a bit hard when he's always around. Wherever I look, there he is. At home. At school. At the field. Everywhere.'

'So, spend less time at home,' he said, as if it was the most obvious answer. And to Tyler, it *was* that simple. Less time at home equalled less time near Rock. An easy maths equation with one answer. 'You could always try and make some other friends if Rock's presence pisses you off that much.'

'And why should I have to do that?' I huffed, crossing my arms in front of my chest. Why should I be the one to have to find new friends? Also, what kind of new friends would I even make? I'd been friends with the other Rebels since we were five.

'We've all been friends for years! That shouldn't have to change just because his mum married my dad.'

'Okay, okay.' He put his hands up to placate me. 'I was just saying, Ari. I'm an answers kind of guy.'

'Yeah, well, don't *just say*.'

An evil glint flashed in Tyler's eyes and I swallowed a gulp of my drink, wondering what the heck he was about to come out with. Knowing Tyler, it was going to be another *answer* that I didn't want to hear.

'You want to make him jealous?' He nudged his head in Rock's direction and I scoffed. Rock had three blonde cheerleaders hanging from his arms and I rolled my eyes at the way they were flirting with him. The way they were acting *so over the top* with him. As if his muscles were worth fawning over the way they were.

'Make him jealous?' I repeated, looking at Tyler again, wondering what stupid shit he was cooking up. 'What you got in mind?'

'Kiss me.'

'Sorry, what?'

'Kiss me,' he said again, his lips curled up into an amused smile.

I weighed up his suggestion in my mind. There was nothing to lose. If Rock saw and didn't give a shit, then at least I knew how he felt about me. Knew that I needed to let the idea of him and me go. Not that there could ever be a 'him and me'. We were family.

'Fine.' I leaned forward, standing on my tiptoes, and cupped Tyler's face with my palms to pull it down to my level. Even on my tiptoes, Tyler was inches taller than me. He towered above us all.

Our lips collided, and at first, we were both gentle. Tentative.

It was weird to be kissing one of my best friends to make my stepbrother jealous, but honestly, stranger things happen daily all over the world. Or so I assumed they did. Didn't have any specifics to back that claim up with or anything.

Tyler was a much better kisser than I expected him to be—not that I'd thought much of kissing Tyler before the moment he suggested it, but once he had, it felt natural. Right.

The longer the kiss lasted, the more involved we both became, with our tongues tangling, hands roaming in that awkward way of two fifteen-year-olds exploring one another for the first time.

I knew Tyler had kissed other girls. Fuck, he'd probably done a lot more than that too, but I'd never been one to mess around with guys.

My heart was holding out for a certain somebody who was off-limits.

Which was a major fucking problem.

Tyler stopped the kiss for a brief second to look at me, his whisper skittering across my face. 'That should do it.'

The pulse in my neck thrummed, my body tight, and the heat of the summer caused my skin to cover in a light sweat sheen. I blinked at Tyler, completely caught up in the moment.

'You think?' I whispered back, his cotton T-shirt underneath my fingertips as they trailed across his back and down to the waistband of his jeans. 'Maybe another one wouldn't hurt.'

His dark blue eyes glinted with mischief and something underlying I couldn't place that disappeared as fast as it arrived.

'You think that's wise?'

'Fuck no,' I said with a small laugh. 'But I'm game if you are?'

'You know me, princess. I'm always game.'

FIVE
ROCK

age 17, august

I LOOKED across the field and was greeted with a sight I didn't think I'd ever see again. One that gutted me the first time but was going to kill me now.

My gut tightened and nausea hit me as I took in the scene.

Arianna and Tyler were kissing.

And fuck, it looked like they meant it this time. The first time they kissed had thrown me, too.

'Whoa!' Spencer called out, raising his beer can in the air. 'Tyler is going in.'

Gray laughed; his arm wrapped around the shoulder of some girl he'd decided was his conquest for the evening. 'Timid Tyler has pulled?'

'I thought he lost the name Timid Tyler after that night he ran through town naked on a dare.'

Gray shrugged, not really giving a fuck either way. Or maybe he didn't want to think about the dares we all got roped into back in those days.

'Who's he necking on now?'

'Arianna!' Spencer's voice was filled with disbelief, but I couldn't see his view because of the people standing in circles dotted around the field and in front of where I'd seen Arianna last.

'Tyler's kissing Arianna?' Gray asked, his tone just as disbelieving.

'You need to get your eyes tested, mate, because there's no way my girl would kiss him.'

'Well, how do you explain that?' Spencer asked, grabbing Gray and moving him to a spot with a better view. I stepped away from the group of girls I'd been chatting with to see what they were looking at and my heart stopped in my chest. Just up and died, right then and there.

Ari was standing with Tyler, exactly as Spencer had said, and the two of them were indeed making out.

What in the actual fuck?

Tyler knew how I felt about her and there was no way he could deny that fact. After all, he was the one I'd opened up to the night of my mum's wedding when I'd had a little too much to drink when I shouldn't have.

What a slimy little prick.

'Looks like you've got some competition,' Gray said, moving to my side and nudging me in the ribs with his sharp elbow.

'I don't know what you're talking about, mate.'

'Bullshit,' he hissed.

I shook my head and looked away from the two of them. The kiss had ended, but they were whispering to one another, their noses practically touching. 'Whatever.'

'You're just gonna take this like a little bitch?'

'She's my stepsister,' I said, as if that explained everything. And to me, it did. Not like our parents would ever approve of the two of us banging under their roof. Or outside of it, either.

'Your loss, mate,' Gray said, shaking his head, clearly thinking I was a fucking idiot.

Yeah, well, join the club.

'Told you the two of them looked cute together,' Sav's cheerful voice said as she came back to stand at my side from wherever she'd been. Usually, I at least gave a shit where she was, but today I didn't care. She could've been off necking someone else in the trees and I wouldn't have given a fuck.

Clearly, I needed to evaluate my relationship. Or should I make that relationships?

I didn't say anything, not wanting Savannah to know she'd hit a nerve, but also because if I showed any outward reaction aside from indifference, she'd rip my head off, or worse, want to have a meaningful and emotional conversation.

Both of which I wasn't ready for.

'Don't you think, babe?' she said, needling me.

'Don't I think what?' I replied, as if the thing she wanted me to comment on wasn't ripping apart my soul piece by piece.

'That Tyler and Arianna make the cutest couple you've ever seen in your life?' She laughed, placing her hand on my chest, her sharp nails scratching my pec in a lazy manner. 'Well, except for us two, of course.'

'I suppose.'

'They look really happy together.'

I blinked, looking back at where the two of them were standing, no longer kissing, but Ari's hands were on his waist and his smile was wide as he looked down at her.

Tyler and I had been friends for a long time, and I knew the majority of his facial expressions. When he was sad, mad, happy, pissed. All of it. And the look on his face as he looked down at Arianna was as genuine as I'd ever seen him give.

Shit.

'I suppose,' I repeated, unable to form new sentences apparently.

'Well, *I'm* happy for them,' she stressed before kissing my cheek. Across the field, Gray caught my eye, having seen what we were looking at, and I shook my head, not wanting to draw any more attention to it. 'Arianna deserves somebody, doesn't she? And who even knows. Maybe the four of us can double date?'

'Why would we do that?'

'Why wouldn't we?' She regarded me with a speculative gaze and I looked away from the question in her eyes. 'She's your sister, he's your mate, and we all go to school together. It's a no-brainer.'

'A no-brainer. Right.'
Double shit.

THE NEXT NIGHT, I was home alone, waiting for Ari to come home from wherever the fuck she was.

By the time I felt ready to approach her and Tyler at the field, the two of them had got the fuck out of dodge, and they didn't come back. Gray reckoned they'd headed to Tyler's flat, but I hoped he was wrong and that he'd been a gentleman and taken Ari home instead.

However, when I came back the morning after to an empty, echoing space, I knew she hadn't returned home all night, meaning Gray was probably right about the two of them going back to Ty's.

By three in the afternoon, I was pacing the entryway, waiting for her return.

Could I just text her? Of course I could, but the two of us didn't have that kind of relationship anymore. Not since what happened last summer.

By five, I was getting pissed.

Then at six, one of the double doors opened and there she was.

'Shit!' she shouted, grabbing her chest with her hand. 'You scared me.'

'Sorry,' I said, still pacing, not wanting to admit to myself just how long I'd been doing so. 'Just wasn't sure what time you'd be home.'

'Right...' she trailed off, stepping inside and closing the door with a gentle click behind her. 'So why didn't you just message me?'

'I didn't know if I could.'

'Huh?'

'I didn't know if your new beau would have an issue with it.' Okay, so not entirely true, but my worry about her was resulting in my anger bubbling to the surface rather than the care about her safety I should be showing.

'What?' Ari placed her bag down at the bottom of the stairs and turned to face me head-on, crossing her arms in her go-to defensive stance. 'Are you seriously pissed at me right now?'

'I suppose I am!'

'Why?' she asked, incredulous. 'You've never cared before.'

'Well, that was before you sucked Tyler's face off!'

'Excuse me? You of all people can't exactly get mad at me kissing somebody.'

'Tyler isn't just *somebody*, though, is he?'

'What does that even mean?'

I could see the exasperation on her face, could see that continuing the conversation was not going to end well, but I couldn't help myself. It was like a compulsion or something. Like every feeling I'd had for her over the last however many years was bubbling to the surface and taking over me.

'It's not like it's the first time the two of you have hooked up. Don't pretend you don't remember that field party back when we were fifteen. It was only a couple years ago!'

'And?'

'So, you can't deny there's something going on between the two of you.' She opened her mouth to interrupt, but I continued. 'Plus, you didn't even come home last night, and you weren't at the field, so that leads to only one conclusion.'

'And what conclusion is that?' she huffed, shuffling her weight to her other leg, arms still crossed.

'That you went back to Tyler's flat with him.'

'So, what if I did? I fail to see how any of it has anything to do with you.'

I took a deep breath, trying to calm myself down, but not doing a very good job of it.

'This is all coming out wrong, Ari. Let me try and start this conversation again.' I took a step towards her, wanting to pull her into my arms, but stopping myself when I remembered that she wasn't mine to touch. Wasn't mine to hold close and whisper sweet nothings to. 'I'm sorry for acting like an arse. I was just worried about you when you didn't come back to the field, and then even more worried when I got home and the house was empty. And then I didn't feel like I could text you because all we do when we talk now is argue and our friendship is basically non-existent.'

'I still want to be your friend, Rock. It's just hard.'

'I know,' I mumbled, taking another step closer to her. 'But everything's just fucked-up and I can't see a way to make it better.'

'Dumping Savannah would be a start,' she blurted. 'Wait, no, I never said that.'

'Funny that, because the words definitely just left your lips,' I attempted to joke, but it fell flat when I saw her face fall. 'Is that what you want?'

'It has nothing to do with what *I* want,' she snapped. 'I'm not the one fucking her.'

'Neither am I.'

'Bullshit. There's no way you're not reaping the benefits of a girlfriend who's obsessed with you.'

She was right, but I didn't want to tell her that. Wasn't even sure why I'd denied it in the first place. Not that I was having sex with Savannah on a daily basis or anything, but we weren't celibate either.

The shame was a lot.

'Rock, go spend the summer with your girlfriend and I'll spend mine with people who care about me.'

'Like Tyler?'

'Like Tyler and Grayson, yes.'

'They don't care about you the way I do!'

'Well, you've got a fucking funny way of showing it, prick.'

She shook her head, mad at herself for even engaging in the argument. I knew Ari. She wasn't the type to let herself get riled up easily. Her shoulders rose as she inhaled, a look of peace covering her features. 'Look. How about we just ignore each other until the festival? Or fuck, after that if need be.'

'That's really what you want? There are another four weeks until Beurrefest.'

'I'm aware.'

'Well…' I looked at her, trying to read something from the closed-off expression on her face but not succeeding. 'Your wish is my command, *princess*.'

'Fine!'

'Fine.'

Six

Arianna

age 15, august

SUMMER ALWAYS FELT like such a chore.

No matter how much I loved being out of school, there was only so long before I got bored of the boys' antics.

Being the only girl took its toll.

'So, what exactly is this festival going to include?' Gray asked one night when all of us were together at the field. Now that Maxwell and his friends weren't lurking around at all hours, the field had become our place. The place we could go and not have to worry about shit.

In the last month or so, the Matthews family had determined that owning the fields meant they had enough space to throw a small summer festival for the local people of Beurre as a way to celebrate Maxwell's life and everything he may have accomplished had he not died. Which, yeah, sure. Let's celebrate a prick.

The very field Maxwell used to hang out in all the time was the perfect place for a festival in his honour, after all, and though we had a party every Friday night at the same spot, it was only a small fraction of the land they owned. According to Samantha Matthews, it going unused all summer was a waste. Although really, she just wanted a reason to further celebrate her oldest son, whose light was dimmed too early—his dazzling life cut short by a crime too horrid to talk about.

The crime may be horrid, but Maxwell Matthews was anything but dazzling.

'Seems like it'll be a laugh whatever it is,' Gray added, a smile fixed on his face, probably thinking the same shitty things about Maxwell as I was.

'Mum's asked some local bands to play, and a couple of circus acts and carnival rides have said they'll come. This year she's selling tickets for cheap, and people will stay the one night if they want to. The field we throw our parties in is going to be where everybody pitches their tents and whatever, and then the other fields will have the stages for music and some tents for other shit like a silent disco and whatnot.'

'Your mum's really going all out,' Rock pointed out, and Spencer nodded.

'Max was her golden child.'

The sadness in that sentence had faded with time, but I knew Spencer still resented the way his family treated his older brother's ghost when compared to how they treated their very much alive son. He'd died a year ago, for fuck's sake, which okay wasn't actually that long ago but still. Poor Spencer.

'And she plans for this to become an annual thing?' I asked, wondering what the catch was.

'Yep. Wants it to get bigger with time so everybody will know the name Maxwell Matthews.'

'Sure Isadora will be thrilled,' Ace said under his breath but still louder than he'd intended.

'Isadora doesn't matter,' Spencer spat, and that was the end of that.

Seven

Arianna

age 17, september

THE FESTIVAL WAS HELD on the first weekend of September, just before school started, and the turnout that first year was relatively small.

Then the next year it grew a little bigger. More kids came. More bands played. More food trucks took up spots.

The third year, tickets were triple the initial cost and people were able to camp the entire weekend—from Friday to Monday—plus, the bands playing were real-world bands and not just ones from the local area. Real artists were fighting to play at the small festival that took over the fields of Beurre at the end of each summer, and people were travelling into town to attend.

It was fucking wild.

And every year, there we all were, ready to celebrate the end of another summer together—all while pretending we gave a shit about the dead kid it was all in memory of.

'Are you ready?' Gray asked when he arrived at mine at lunchtime on the Friday to travel to the field with me. 'Got everything you need?'

'Gray, the field's a walk away. Not like we can't return at any point during the weekend if need be. If I've forgotten anything, I can always demand one of my dad's lackeys to bring it to me, anyway.'

'Oh, the benefits of wealth,' he joked, but maybe it wasn't much of a joke to him. I was too chickenshit to ask what he really thought about it all. Money had never come between us before, and I wouldn't let it happen now. 'Let's go do this shit.'

'Can't wait.'

'Reckon she'll continue to throw this every year until she dies?'

'Or until someone else does, yeah.'

Gray nodded thoughtfully. It was only a matter of time until somebody overdosed or something at the field and the festival would be no more.

'Imagine if Max could see all this,' Gray said with a small laugh. 'He'd be in his element.'

'It really does suck that he sucked. I hate thinking poor of the dead.'

'Just because somebody's dead, it doesn't mean they were a good person, right? So, we don't have to sugarcoat shit. Especially not with each other. We're best friends, Ree. You never have to pretend with me.'

'No, I know,' I said and meant it. I knew Gray had my back the same way I would always have his. Our friendship was forged from such a young age that I couldn't possibly imagine my life without him in it, constantly at my side. 'Have you got everything you need?'

'If you mean booze, then yeah, I've got plenty. Hid some bottles in a Pringles tube and ev.'

'Cool beans. Spencer said his mum's ramped up the security this year because of the attendance levels.'

'And because the police in town can only overlook *so* much.'

We laughed. The cops in town overlooked a fucking lot as it was, but because the festival had gained traction and even a spot on a national television morning news show, the police needed to be seen to be doing their job correctly. For once.

'Is everyone else meeting us there?'

'Think so. Ace said he and Tyler were getting there early to help set up the signs and that.' Grayson shrugged. 'What about Rock?'

I shivered at the mention of my stepbrother. The wanker.

'Why would I know what his plans are?'

'Because you live in the same house… He's a part of your family, whether you like it or not.'

It was my turn to shrug.

'He may live here, but you know we don't talk.'

'Maybe—'

'No,' I snapped. 'He has his life and I have mine. Let's keep it that way.'

'He has a girlfriend, Ree. That shouldn't make him dead to you.'

'Whatever.' I flicked my hair over my shoulder, ever the princess, and ignored anything else Gray said about Rock and his *girlfriend* the entire journey to the field.

THE FESTIVAL WAS the same as always.

Kind of.

Everyone in our group had pitched their tents together in a circle, with a large space in the centre for us all to sit and lounge around, a spot made for drinking and playing games.

'Paranoid!' Savannah called out and my body reacted to her shrill voice as it cut across the circle. My lips turned up into a smile, though. Of course she was paranoid. Gray knew what he was doing when he'd whispered his question into my ear.

Who do you think is the most likely to pass out drunk this weekend?

I made sure to reply with a wicked glint in my eye as I surveyed the circle before answering. *Savannah.*

Paranoid wasn't a game for the weak.

You sat in a circle and in turns the person to your right would whisper a question in your ear. One that had a one-word answer: somebody else's name.

The person you named could choose whether to let it slide and never find out the whispered question, and the two people asking and answering the question could drink, or they could shout paranoid, take a drink, and find out the question for themselves—well, them and everyone else playing the game.

Sometimes people would get peer pressured into shouting paranoid, just because somebody else playing wanted to know the question.

Gray had asked me a relatively easy question, but the bastard had asked knowing I would name Savannah as my answer. He wanted to make her paranoid. And Rock too.

I have the best best friend.

'You really want to know?' Gray asked, laughing as he took a sip of his vodka. Rock glared at us both and I couldn't hold in my giggle.

'I do,' Savannah replied, readying her drink to take a sip. 'Arianna looks evil.'

'Thanks,' I said, laughing more. It was either laugh or reach across the circle and slap her, and for that moment I didn't choose violence.

'I asked her who she thought was going to pass out drunk this weekend. And if you keep shouting paranoid every time somebody says your name, you're going to make it come true. Time to drink up.'

'Is that really what you asked?' Savannah asked, her voice small and unsure. Like she'd been caught out. Or maybe she thought we were lying to her.

'We're not liars,' Gray said. 'We take the honesty and integrity of Paranoid seriously, I'll have you know.'

The entire circle broke out into laughter then, and Savannah took a drink, mollified but quiet.

Rock rubbed her knee in reassurance, and I saw red.

Well, actually, I saw the world in a tan tint as I was wearing my sunglasses, but still.

The girl boiled my blood just because she existed, and there was literally fuck all I could do about it.

Not like I was going to tell Rock how I felt about him.

No way, no how.

'My turn!' I announced, turning to whisper in Tyler's ear, who was sitting to my left. There were some girls in the circle that I didn't know, but the others all seemed to. I lowered my voice to a whisper. 'What girl do you find the most attractive in the circle?'

He narrowed his eyes and looked at me, trying to read something on my face, but I didn't move a muscle.

'Arianna,' he replied, looking me in the eye and not removing it even when the circle started to cry out that he couldn't name the person asking the question.

'Why not?' he asked, still looking at me. 'Nothing in the rules that says I can't.'

'But she's not gonna say she's paranoid because she knows the question!' Ace said, and everyone else nodded, knowing the boy had spoken sense.

'So, either we both drink,' Tyler said, 'or Ari asks me something else.'

'Or you could answer somebody else,' I pointed out, not wanting to think too hard about his answer. He probably just meant it in a, you're the best looking outta the bunch but not like that, kind of way. Or at least I hoped he did.

'I take the honesty and integrity of Paranoid seriously, I'll have you know,' he joked, copying Gray's words from before.

'Fine,' I gritted out, and we both took a sip of our drinks, his eyes still locked on mine, his smile causing butterflies to flutter in my stomach.

Down, girl.

'THAT WAS A WILD GAME.'

I looked up and saw Tyler's head—and only his head—the rest of his body still outside my tent, and laughed. In the space of two hours, I'd drunk a lot more than I should've.

'Paranoid always brings out the best, and worst, in everyone.' I chuckled and went back to arranging my sleeping bag on the floor of the tent. I was sharing with Gray and somehow we'd managed to secure a large four-person tent, rather than the pissing pop-up he usually had for things like this.

It had taken us a long time to put it up the day before in comparison to how easy the pop-up was, but it had all been worth it for the space we'd had during the night.

'Are you hungry?' he asked, stepping into the tent fully, a wide smile on his face. 'The toastie place is back this year.'

'The one that does cheese and caramelised onion?' I screeched, my stomach grumbling as I did so. I hadn't thought about food until Tyler mentioned it, but the moment he'd put it out into the universe, I was all of a sudden ravenous.

'The very one.'

'Fuck, I want that.'

'Thought you would.' He rubbed his jaw, the smile still firm on his face.

He looks really pretty when he smiles.

No, no, no.

I thought I'd agreed with myself that I wasn't going there… again.

'Want me to grab you a toastie and bring it back, or you want to come with me?'

'Who's out there?' I nudged my head in the direction of the circle I'd left drinking and playing ring of fire.

'Rock and Savannah. Oh, and Sav's friends.'

'Yeah, fuck that. I'll come with you.'

'That's what I was hoping you'd say.'

I rolled my eyes, hoping the blush on my cheeks wasn't that apparent.

'Where's Gray?'

'Off with some girl, I think.' He shrugged. 'You know what the boy's like.'

'That I do.'

My stomach grumbled again, even louder, and I grimaced.

'Let's go get you food.'

'Let's.'

EIGHT
ROCK

age 17, september

EVER SINCE ARIANNA told me she didn't want to speak to me, I'd done my best to stay away from her the entire summer.

With our parents recently returned home, it was a little harder to avoid her completely, but even if she did speak to me at meals and shit, it was boring stuff like: *could you pass the gravy?* Or something like: *I'll call for more wine.* Or my personal favourite: *how's your meat cooked, Rock?*

Proper mundane and unimportant shit.

But now we were both at Beurrefest, camping in the tents next to each other, and I knew I'd jump on the opportunity to talk to her without her getting mad. Even if other people were there to witness, and listen to, every conversation we had.

All I wanted was to get her alone, away from everybody and everything, but I knew that wasn't possible.

I was a prick for even wanting that in the first place.

You have a girlfriend, I repeated in my head anytime I even thought of Arianna in a romantic way. Or in any way other than the way I should be feeling about a sibling, even if she was only a stepsibling and there was no blood between us.

I'd watched as Tyler took Arianna off, alone, to grab some

food, and my stomach muscles clenched at the view, but there was nothing I could do about it.

She'd made her choice and so had I.

'I really think the two of them are more serious than we first thought, you know?'

Savannah's voice grated as she whispered in my ear and I nodded, knowing that if I replied, my voice would give my inner turmoil away.

'They sneak off all the time, and she always smiles so bright whenever he's around. I wonder if they kick Grayson out of the tent tonight.'

'Why would they do that?'

'For some privacy, silly.' She lightly slapped my arm, a teasing expression on her face, and my jaw clenched. 'Not like they'll get much here, though. Did you hear the noises from Remi's tent?'

'Nope,' I said. 'Didn't think she was camping near us.'

'Neither did I...' Sav shrugged. 'Maybe she isn't and whoever she's hooked up with is the person near us.'

'I thought she was into Dean Walters still. When did they split up?'

'Beginning of summer, I think? I don't know for definite. Not like I'd ever ask her. I can't stand the girl.'

'She's not that bad.'

'You're just saying that,' she replied within seconds. 'But everybody knows she's a massive bitch who doesn't deserve any friends.'

'That's a bit harsh,' I said, not voicing whether I agreed with her or not—mainly because I'd never put enough thought into it. I knew that Tyler and Spencer had their issues with Remi, but me personally? I'd never had a reason to dislike her. Maybe if she'd acted shitty to Arianna I'd feel differently about her, but as far as I knew, she never had.

'Whatever.' Savannah shrugged, taking her lips away from

my ear and moving so I could see her fully. 'You're just a nice guy.'

'Is there a problem with being nice?'

'No…' she trailed off, looking around the now-empty circle. 'Where did everybody go?'

'To get lunch, I guess. You want anything?'

She made a disgusted sound at the back of her throat. 'All the food here has been grim and super greasy.'

'Right…' I shook my head, wondering how the fuck I'd found myself in my current position. 'So do you want anything?'

'Of course I do!' she said, a bright but strained smile on her lips. 'Otherwise, I'll be eating nothing.'

'Maybe there's something healthy somewhere. A salad bar or something.'

'Maybe.' But from the look on her face, I could tell she wasn't convinced.

LUCKY FOR US, Savannah was able to find something to eat that she didn't sneer at, so it was a win for me.

By the time we made it back to the tents, everybody had returned and was sitting around in a circle, a speaker and dirty pint cup in the centre, playing a large group game of Ring of Fire.

'Rock!' Spencer called, ushering us over, a cup in his outstretched hand. 'Come join us!'

'Maybe in a minute,' I called back, heading over to Savannah's and my tent. My thoughts went back to the previous day, back to when we were all arriving and setting up our tents, and how little Savannah had helped me.

She'd opened up a camping chair, poured herself a cup of

vodka and lemonade, and sat laughing and joking with her friends while I did all the work.

When I'd looked over to see Arianna helping Grayson with theirs, my gut twinged—for probably the thirtieth fucking time since arriving—and I wondered where I'd gone wrong.

Somehow, somewhere along the line, I'd ended up with the wrong girl.

God, I'm a cunt.

I knew exactly when things had changed and how I'd ended up with the wrong girl, and it all started on the first night of Beurrefest the year before...

NINE
ROCK

age 16, september

'Do you think there's a chance?' I asked, looking deep into Arianna's jade green eyes.

The noise from our friends filtered into the tent we were sitting in, but I ignored it, putting all my focus on her. Arianna deserved all the focus to be on her.

Things between us since we'd become stepsiblings had been sour, to say the least, and I knew it was mostly my fault.

'A chance of what?'

'A chance for us?'

My whisper permeated through the available space in the tent, and I held my breath, scared and apprehensive about her reply. It was the first time I'd uttered something like that to her, but I couldn't bring myself to take it back.

The two of us had pussyfooted around one another for years, and the alcohol running through me was giving me the courage I'd never had before.

'I—' Ari looked around the tent, finding nowhere to focus her gaze, so she turned back to look me in the eye. 'I thought you didn't feel it.'

'It?'

'The chemistry between us,' she said, blinking slowly. 'You've never given me the impression that you like me like that or anything.'

'Shit, Ari, I've always fancied you.'

'Huh?'

'Since we were like ten, I've had a crush on you. Shit, maybe even younger than that.'

Her laughter was loud, and her hair tickled my hand as I ran my fingers along her cheek.

'What's so funny?' I asked, resting my hand on her chin, pulling her face up so we were eye to eye, nose to nose.

'What's funny is that I've had a crush on you for-literal-ever and the moment you became my stepbrother was one of the saddest because I knew then that we could never even see what we could be.'

I ignored the end of her sentence, not wanting to accept she'd written us off so spectacularly before we'd ever tried, and focused on the start. 'You have?'

'Of course I have. Why do you think I've avoided you for the last couple years?'

'I just thought you were pissed my mum married your dad and you were taking it out on me.'

'Oh.' She shook her head. 'No, that's not it at all.'

'Oh.'

We both fell silent, the sounds of our friends' laughter filling the small inch of space between us. While talking, our faces had come closer together, and I could see every freckle on her nose. Every individual eyelash that framed her beautiful eyes.

'How much have you had to drink?' she asked in a whisper, breaking the silence. 'Because I've drunk *a lot* and I'm worried you have too, and that's the only reason you're saying the words you're saying.'

'A little.'

'I watched you down an entire dirty pint in one gulp.'

'Well, yeah, but that doesn't mean I don't know what I'm saying, does it?'

'You tell me.'

'That *was* me telling you.' I laughed, finding every single thing about her adorable. I always had. 'Want me to spell it out in interpretive dance or some shit?'

'I'd pay to see that.' Her laughter joined mine. 'Maybe you should spell it out, just to make sure I understand.'

I moved a fraction—a bluff—but Arianna's hand darted out to stop me, landing on my thigh. My dick twitched, wanting so bad to join the party, but knowing she was off-limits. That the only hand he had to look forward to was my own. *What a depressing fucking thought.*

'Don't move,' she hushed out, her breath fanning out across my cheeks. 'I'm not ready to leave this moment.'

'I wasn't going anywhere.'

'Good.'

Ten

Arianna

age 16, september

'I'M NOT ready to leave this moment.' My words were a low hush in the tent, and I was glad that the lighting was pretty dim. Otherwise, Rock would be able to see the blush slowly bleeding across my face and down my neck to my chest.

The moment he'd moved, my heart had stopped, and I thought I'd lost him. Thought he was going to walk away from me, and that would be that.

If he left, there would be no revisiting. No way to claw it back.

'I wasn't going anywhere,' he replied, his earnest eyes gutting me in the best way.

My heart's rhythm picked up once more, stuttering back to the fast pace it was before he moved.

'Good.'

All I had to do was lean forward, just an inch, and our lips would touch. Would brush together and become the kiss I'd wanted for a *really* long time. It would finally happen and I could die happy.

But I wasn't sure if I could bring myself to actually make the move. What if he rejected me? What if it was all in my head and he didn't like me the way I liked him?

'Ari?'

'Yes.'

'Kiss me.' His large eyes were aglow in the dark light of the tent, and I swallowed, my nerves reaching a crescendo. When it became clear I was frozen to the spot, unable to move even a centimetre closer, Rock took the initiative and closed the gap between us. His lips touched mine as his strong arms came around me to hold me close, and I melted.

Melted into a puddle right then and there.

The kiss was tentative at first, neither of us quite believing we were crossing the line we'd held in place for so long. No matter how long I'd wanted to kiss him, I never thought it would become reality. Especially not in a tent with all our friends in the surrounding ones.

'Are you okay?' he whispered, breaking the kiss to look at me. 'We can stop?'

'No,' I whispered. 'I don't want to stop.'

'Are you sure?'

'I'm sure.' I smiled, blinking at him, wanting him to stop talking and get back to kissing me. 'Kiss me, Rock.'

Rock crushed his mouth to mine, his hunger calling to my own in an instant. While our kiss intensified, his body pressed against mine, moving us so I was lying beneath him. He devoured me like a starving man, biting at my lips, and a sharp emotion I didn't want to focus on ran through me. He caught my bottom lip and pulled just enough to make me feel at his mercy for a moment.

Rock broke our kiss and I tried to pull him back down, but his strength meant I had no chance. 'Ari, we should talk about this.'

'I don't want to *talk*,' I said, emphasis aplenty. 'Now get back here.'

Rock still looked unsure.

What can I do to convince him this is what I want?

Ah!

I sat up and in one swift movement, I pulled my top off over my head before moving my hands around to unlatch my bra, letting it fall to the tent floor when done. Then it was time for me to remove my leggings, so I was lying there with only my knickers left on. I wasn't ready just yet to remove them without encouragement.

Once I was settled once more with my back on the camping mattress, Rock pulled off his shirt, my hunger rising as I took in his super muscular frame. He'd always lifted weights and been fucking hot, but seeing him like this, vulnerable and alone, it hit home just how perfect he was.

Kneeling by my feet, he looked over my body, a contemplative expression on his face. The tent was getting hotter, or maybe it was just me?

I'd wanted him to look at me that way for ages, and the fact he finally was made my stomach drop out from beneath me.

Anticipation went through me in waves when Rock pulled my legs apart, allowing him access to all of me. 'You're beautiful, Arianna.'

A blush came over me as he leaned over, kissing and nibbling my legs first, thankfully allowing me to relax a little by the time he got to the edge of my lace knickers.

I needed to calm down—and fast.

'I'm asking again,' he whispered, his eyes reaching mine from where he was positioned between my legs, 'because I respect you more than anything in this world, Ari. Are you sure you want to go all the way with me?'

'Have you ever…' I trailed off, unsure if I even wanted to know the answer to the finished question.

'No,' he replied, answering anyway, moving to come rest over me, his elbows propping him up. 'I always hoped it would be you.'

'Oh.'

'Have you? Done this before, I mean.'

'No.' My whisper was nearly drowned out by the shouts of

our friends outside the tent and it pulled me back to the moment, reminding me where we were. 'I suppose I always hoped it would be you, too.'

His Adam's apple bobbed as he swallowed, the lust in his eyes ramping up at my admission.

'You mean that?'

I nodded, coming to rest my forehead on his, locking our gazes together.

Rock's fingers trailed down my body. Tingles followed at each patch of skin he touched, and I hissed out a breath, wanting more.

His hand reached the line of my underwear. His eyes were seeking permission, but didn't he realise he'd asked for enough permission already?

How many more ways could I say yes to him?

How many more times could I say yes?

So, I took control of the situation.

I moved my hand from his shoulder and placed it where his was lingering above my pubis, ready to breach my underwear. Together, we moved his hand to where we both wanted it most.

'Shit,' I moaned as his fingers went between my wet folds and made contact. 'Shit, Rock.'

'Are you okay?'

'Put your finger inside me,' I demanded, not wanting to answer him and ruin the moment slowly building between us. I loved that he wanted to check that I was okay and still wanted this with him, but fuck, he needed to stop talking and take action. 'Now.'

The moment his finger penetrated me, I gasped, not surprised by the intrusion but also surprised by it at the same time. Did that even make sense? Fuck if I knew. I was delirious, trapped in a lust-fuelled haze I never wanted to return from.

He added a second finger, then a third, and with each added digit, I climbed even higher to the point where there was nowhere for me to go but over the edge.

'Come over my fingers, Ari,' he breathed in my ear, and I grabbed his wrist with a death grip.

My eyes rolled back as I let the need building inside of me take over to the point where I wasn't in my body anymore. It was as if I was watching it all unfold from above, a shadow hidden in the darkness.

When I came back to myself, Rock was gazing deep into my eyes, a look of awe flecked in his own, his dick now lined up with my entrance, ready to take the plunge.

Before he could open his mouth and ask once more if I was sure, I used my hand still between us to help push him inside, little by little, until he was fully seated inside of me.

The sting hurt, but not as much as I'd thought it would, or maybe it was the fact I was so ready for this moment to pass I was dissociating with it. Small mercies and all that. I kissed his lips, our foreheads pressed together, and smiled tentatively. 'It's okay for you to move,' I whispered.

'Okay.'

At first, he moved slow, not wanting to hurt me, but once he realised I wasn't about to break beneath him, he picked up his pace.

The feel of him inside me was more than I'd bargained for, and it sent me to a new level of wanting him.

Of needing him.

Fuck. Fuck. Fuck.

'Shit, Ari, I'm gonna come if you don't soon.'

'Charming.' The breathless giggle that left my lips took us both by surprise—mostly because it made my walls tighten and the sensation even better, as if that were possible.

'Do it again,' he said, thrusting harder. I laughed, and it sent us both over the edge, my moans increasing in both speed and volume.

He clapped his hand over my mouth before I could scream out his name, too lost in the emotions to remember where we were.

My walls contracted as he spilled himself inside of me. Thank fuck I was on the pill. Otherwise, other thoughts would be rushing through my mind, but the only thought I could muster was *doesn't he look so fucking sexy hovering over me.*

Rock kissed me so hard I thought it may leave a bruise, stilling himself before pulling out of me. 'Are you okay?'

'Never better,' I told him, meaning it, placing a kiss on his cheek before moving to his lips. 'That was… fuck, Rock, that was amazing.'

It was just a shame it was a one-off and couldn't lead anywhere more.

WE AWOKE IN THE TENT, tangled up in one another, and a deep wash of shame and regret trickled through me.

I didn't regret sleeping with Rock, and I didn't feel shame at losing my virginity to the guy I'd always wanted to lose it to.

No. I felt shame and regret at what my next actions were going to be. At the way I was going to push him away for our own good, even after last night being the best night of my life.

'Morning,' he murmured, the hand resting on my waist squeezing me closer.

'Morning,' I croaked. 'Are you okay?'

'I should be asking you the same thing.' His smile cut me, causing tiny lesions on my heart, leaking tiny drops of blood through the gaps. 'Last night was amazing, Ari.'

'It was.' I swallowed.

'What are we going to tell our parents?'

'Huh?'

'What are we going to say to our parents?'

'Why the fuck are we telling them anything?' *Have I missed something?* 'You wanna tell my dad we've had sex?'

'Fuck no,' he said with a deep chuckle, still holding me close. 'I meant about us being in a relationship.'

'Us being in a relationship?' I echoed after apparently having turned into a parrot since waking.

'Yeah,' Rock said, his head in a different place than mine. 'Maybe we'll need to keep it quiet for now, but in a year or two we could tell them the truth and—'

'And what?' I interrupted, not wanting to listen anymore to his version of the future, because if I listened too hard, I'd see it and want it to become reality. 'We ride off into the sunset together?'

'Not quite…'

'And what? You're happy to hide for the next year or two?'

'If that's what it takes.'

'Well, I'm not prepared to do that.'

'Not prepared to do *what*?'

'Hide our feelings from our loved ones, or from anyone, because you know what this town's like. There are no secrets here in Beurre—not for long. Somebody would spot us or see something and blab our business to whoever will listen.'

'People can be discreet, you know?'

'Not here, they can't. And I don't want to live my life like that, either. I respect myself, and you, too much to put either of us through it.'

'So, what exactly are you saying here?' Rock's gaze narrowed, assessing my face, and I looked away, no longer able to hold his eye without immense guilt. 'Because it's starting to sound like you don't want to be together.'

'It's not that I don't want to be with you.'

'What is it then?'

'I don't want to hide anything. I don't want to have to lie to people and just constantly cover shit up, and you shouldn't want that for us either.'

'Now you're telling me what I should want?'

'Rock.' His name came out as a whine and I winced inwardly at how I sounded. 'Don't be like that.'

'Arianna,' he mumbled, his tone rising, 'what we did last night was what I've always wanted. It was perfect and I want nothing more than to make this work with you, yet you seem to be backing out of the challenge before it's even started.'

'The fact you used the word challenge isn't helping.'

'Life's hard enough as it is. Why would you deny us what we want? Just explain it to me in a way I'll understand.'

'I'm trying!' Frustration hummed under my skin, annoyed he wanted more from me, but also annoyed at myself for putting myself in the position where the conversation needed to be had. 'I don't want to have to hide. I don't want to have to lie. I don't want to be with you as we won't be together, not really. It will be stolen glances and hidden touches in the dark, and I don't want to live my life like that!'

'It would only be until we turn eighteen and can move out. That's only just over a year away!'

'A year too long,' I said, my shoulders rising and falling along with my deep breathing, trying to stay calm but failing pretty hard. 'Last night was amazing, but we can't repeat it. I think our timing is off.'

'You're being serious right now?'

'Yes.'

'And there's nothing I can say to change your mind?'

'No,' I admitted softly. 'There isn't.'

'Fuck,' he shouted, moving away from me to sit up, covering himself with the sleeping bag. 'I knew you could act like an ice queen, but I never thought you were this much of a stone-cold bitch.'

I let his words wash over me, bathing in his anger and hating myself all the more for letting him down. For allowing myself to sabotage something that could lead to something beautiful.

'Rock.'

'No, I don't want to hear it anymore! I thought last night

meant something to you. Meant we were both accepting a relationship would be hard, but that our happiness was more important than what other people thought, but maybe I should've checked before we fucked because clearly, we weren't on the same wavelength and we never have been!'

'Rock, I'm sorry b—'

'No, Arianna. *I'm* sorry. I'm sorry for letting things get so out of hand between us. Don't worry, you've made your feelings clear. You don't have to worry anymore. I'll leave you the fuck alone the way you want.'

He stood, dressed with anger, then left me alone in the tent. Still naked, covered by the sleeping bag, with tears I allowed to fall once he was gone.

Rejecting him broke my heart. Destroyed me in a way I hadn't expected. Yet there was no taking it back.

I wasn't sure how long I stayed in the tent crying silent tears, but it was long enough that Grayson came and found me. He took one look at me and stayed silent, wrapping his arm around my shoulders to pull me closer to him, letting me cry into his side. He didn't say anything and neither did I.

I wasn't sure what I'd done in a previous life to get him as my best friend, but whatever it was, it was the best thing I'd ever done.

Eleven

Arianna

age 17, september

'Can you believe it's our one-year anniversary?' Savannah asked me, patting Rock's arm, a broad smile on her face.

'No,' I said, blunt and bored. 'I can't.'

'Me neither!' she squealed. 'It feels like just yesterday that we met at this very festival.'

'You met a year ago,' I pointed out. 'You literally got together the day you met, you fucking weirdos.'

Shit. I'd clearly had too much to drink if I was speaking so freely to them both about their relationship. I usually saved my rancour for times I spent with Grayson.

'Well, _I_ think it's romantic,' Savannah said and kissed Rock's cheek, leaving a small smudge of lipstick there that I then couldn't take my eye off of.

That lipstick smudge was mocking me.

Making me want to harm her.

Something I rarely wanted to do. _Okay, so I'm lying to myself these days. What the fuck is new?_

'And clearly, Boo does too. Otherwise, he wouldn't have asked me out the weekend we met.'

Rock rubbed his temple and looked off into the distance, his face half aglow from the floodlights that were dotted around the area.

I bit my tongue. *Boo* and I both knew the real reason he'd asked her out that weekend, and there was nothing romantic about it.

What kind of a nickname was Boo anyway?

Savannah said it had to do with the fact that Rock sounded stupid, and he hated the name Drew, but Boo rhymed with that and it was *cute*.

Nobody thought to mention to her that he was called Rock because he'd always been one of the tallest of our group, and the one with the biggest muscles, but whatever. If she wanted to call a dude who looked like that *Boo*, then I wasn't going to be the one to stop her.

Even if we all thought she was a tad odd for it. Just a tad…

'Well, I'm happy for the two of you,' I lied. 'But I can hear Tyler calling my name so… off I fuck.'

Was Tyler really calling my name? No.

But did I do it on purpose because I knew Tyler's name would piss off Rock more than anybody else's? Yes.

I never said I was nice all the time.

'See you later, Ree!' Savannah called and I bristled. How dare she take my nickname from Gray and use it as if she owned it? Stupid cow. She already had *Boo*; did she really need to take more from me?

God, being drunk made me dramatic. And bitchy. Who knew.

Tyler walked into my path and I smiled, glad it was him and not Gray, who would start asking me questions I didn't want to answer.

'You okay?' he asked, looking behind me at the happy couple I'd just left.

'You know me. I'm always golden.'

'Well, that's how I know you're lying.'

'Huh?'

'You always bullshit when you're not okay. It's your tell.'

'My tell? Really?'

'Yep. Everyone has one.'

'Okay, master. Tell me more.'

'Sure,' he said, reaching out his arm and looping it through mine to pull me along with him back towards the tents. 'I can always tell when Rock is lying, either to himself or others, because he rubs his temple and looks away.'

'I don't believe that.'

'Well, you should. He did it while Savannah was talking just now, didn't you see?'

I didn't admit that I had because that could result in me getting my hopes up and that was stupid. *I* was stupid.

He'd made his choice, and he'd been with that choice for a year, so clearly, he wasn't as unhappy as Tyler believed him to be.

'And what about you?' I cocked a brow, looking up into his gorgeous blue eyes. They weren't bright like Grayson's, but more of a deep blue that set them apart from other people. 'What do you do when you're full of shit?'

'Oh, that's easy.' He rubbed his fingers along mine, soothing. 'I change my tell every time, so that nobody can figure it out.'

'But isn't the whole point of a tell the fact you don't even realise you're doing it? It's involuntary.'

'I suppose.' His lips tilted up into a secretive smile. 'But I guess I'm always conscious of my lies as I say them.'

'And do you lie often?' I tapped my foot on the floor, prodding his tense chest with my finger. 'Because that's what it sounds like.'

'Not to you,' he deflected. 'Never to you.'

'Make sure it stays that way.'

'Anything you say, princess.'

'WHAT ARE YOU DOING HERE?'

I blinked, the bright lights of the carnival rides lit up the darkness in flashes, causing my eyes to struggle with... well... whatever the hell I was looking at.

'Huh?' I asked, dazed and slightly drunk.

'What are you doing here?' Rock repeated, coming into view looking as devastatingly handsome as always, the sly fucker.

'Here as in Beurrefest? Or here as in the carnival?' I looked behind him, thinking I might spot Savannah, but it seemed he was alone. *Never good.* I worked hard to stay away from being alone with him and at a place like this, with the drink flowing, nothing good could come of it.

'The carnival,' he said, his tone telling me he thought I was acting dumb. 'Why are you alone?'

'Tyler went off to get some snacks.' I gestured in the general direction Tyler had headed off in around ten minutes before.

'You didn't want to go with him?'

I shook my head. 'Nope. Would rather watch the waltzers and see how many people come off green.'

He laughed at that. 'Got any pukers yet?'

'Only the one.' I pointed discreetly over to the other side of the path to a girl who was as pale as a sheet, hunched over, her friend soothing her back. 'She told the workers to stop, which of course meant they made her go faster.'

'Of course.' He chuckled harder. 'Why would anybody in their right mind tell a waltzer spinner to *stop*? It only spurs them on.'

'I know right.' We shook our heads, both still looking in the direction of the poor girl who'd finally moved to an upright position so her friends could shuffle her back to her tent, or to wherever they were headed next. Rock and I fell silent, moving our gaze back to the waltzers where another ride session had started. The music was blaring and the lights were flashing, and honestly, the whole thing made me smile wide. 'What are you doing here anyway?'

'Here as in?'

'The waltzers. Alone.'

'I'm not alone,' he said, a cheeky grin making my knees weak. 'I'm with you.'

'So you are.'

I looked around, hoping Ty's head would come into view—or the head of any Rebel for that matter, but alas, I was unlucky. Other than some teens younger than us, there wasn't anybody else around.

'Makes me wonder,' he started, taking a step closer to me. My breath hitched, my eyes lost in his, no longer looking around for my rescue. 'Whether you'd rather be alone.'

'Rather than what?'

'Than being stuck alone, in the dark, with me.'

'We're not in the dark,' I pointed out, my throat bobbing as I swallowed. 'We're standing by the brightest ride known to man.'

'Ah,' he said, tilting his head down to mine, 'but we are alone.'

'The workers are staring at us,' I said blankly, my tone uninterested, while my skin was on fire. Literal fire. Everything about Rock's piercing gaze was causing me to overheat, and yet he came a step closer, probably all while knowing the effect he had on me.

'They're probably staring at the flush on your face,' he said in a conversational tone. As if I wasn't standing there dying right in front of his eyes. 'It makes your eyes stand out even more than usual.'

'Thanks…' I trailed off, going up on the balls of my feet to see if I could spot *anyone* that would save me. *Still nobody around.* How fucking grand. 'Shouldn't you be off somewhere private with your *girlfriend?*'

Okay. Maybe it wasn't the smartest thing to do, bringing up Savannah and all, but I felt I had no choice. The boy had backed me into a corner—figuratively for the time being—and I needed an escape route. Anything would do.

'My girlfriend's off with her friends,' he said, his voice melting my insides. Fuck. Fuck. Fuck. 'Something about needing to go to town for supplies.'

'She's not here?' I whispered, then coughed, clearing my throat so my next words didn't come out quite so breathless. 'I mean, she's left the campsite?'

He nodded, a smirk playing on his lips. 'Yep.'

'Oh.'

'It's just me and you, ice queen. Isn't that what you wanted?'

'No.' I moved a step back, away from his personal bubble, holding back a sigh. 'I never want that.'

'That's a shame,' he said, closing the distance between us again, and honestly, I wasn't sure if I had much restraint to keep stepping back. Not just at that moment, but in life in general. I was always fighting my feelings for Rock. Always backing myself into a literal corner. Yet I never seemed to learn my lesson.

Stupid girl.

'Shame?' I repeated, my tongue tied to the point it seemed I couldn't do anything but utter his word back at him.

'Shame.' He nodded, his dark brown eyes drawing me in. The flick of his tongue as he licked his bottom lip was near enough to send me over the edge, but I stood my ground.

He has a girlfriend, I told myself. *He doesn't want to be with you.*

But that wasn't true, was it?

It was *me* who had rejected *him*.

'I think we should head back to the tents and find the others.' I swished my head, my ponytail moving with me, and looked to the path that headed back to the campsite. 'They're probably wondering where we've got to.'

'Nobody is at the tents,' Rock said. 'They've all gone elsewhere.'

'Okay then, so…' Guess we wouldn't be heading back there anytime soon. Me, Rock, and a tent wasn't a good idea. No, scratch that. It was one of the *worst* ideas.

'Let's head back to the tents.' Rock's eyes gleamed with malice, but his tone was teasing.

'No way, mister!' A couple of passersby stared at my shout and I paused to take a deep breath. 'I mean. No, Rock. We're not going back to the empty campsite alone.'

'Why?' He chuckled. 'Worried about being alone with me in a tent? Worried it'll bring back memories?'

I gulped, neither confirming nor denying his suspicions. 'I told Tyler I'd wait for him here.'

'Do you like him or something?'

'Tyler?' Rock nodded, crossing his large arms over his chest, drawing my eyes to his muscles. 'Of course I like Tyler.'

'You know I don't mean it like that.'

'Well, I have no idea how you *do* mean it.' I shrugged, the picture of nonchalance and airiness. 'Ty's one of my best friends. Just like Gray and just like you.'

'You've never kissed Gray.' Rock rubbed his jaw, and it wasn't until that moment that I realised how close he was standing. There was barely an inch separating us anymore. *When the fuck had he managed that?* 'But you've kissed Tyler and you've kissed me. So do you like Tyler as more than a friend or not?'

'I'm not going to dignify your needling with an answer.' I imitated his crossed arms and stamped my foot too for good measure. The wanker thought he could get the best of me, but I wasn't going to let him. 'Now, if you'll leave me alone, I can go back to enjoying the bright lights and puking people.'

I took a step back, ready to move to a different section entirely just to get away from him and the way he was making me feel.

It was as if the air was supercharged between us at all times and there was no fucking escape.

'Arianna.'

It was one word. Only one. But Rock somehow managed to put a lot of meaning behind it. Enough that it made me stop and look up into his eyes. *Really* look into them.

Something I should never, ever, ever do.

'Fuck it.' I strode forward, closing the small gap I'd created, and grabbed his hand to pull him back into the darkness. From where we'd moved to, we were hidden from anybody strolling past, and I felt bold.

And like a bitch at the same time.

A bold bitch.

One who was about to throw caution to the wind and kiss their stepbrother. Their totally *not* single stepbrother.

It wasn't even like I could blame it on the alcohol running through my veins—which did exist—because I hated people that used drink as an excuse for their shittier actions.

'What are you doing?' he asked, his mouth opened in surprise at me.

'Just shut up and kiss me.'

His eyes turned questioning. He was giving me a chance to change my mind, to back out of the stupid position I'd put us in and walk away. Dignity still intact.

But I didn't do that.

No. I moved closer, went up on my tiptoes, gripped his chin with my thumb and pointer finger, and pressed my lips against his.

'This is a bad idea,' he whispered against my lips.

'The worst ever,' I agreed. 'But doesn't that make it so much more fun?'

The moment the words left my lips, I realised I meant them. Every fibre in my being was alive with the forbidden quality of it all. With the fact he was taken and I was his stepsister and fuck, maybe my head needed inspecting.

Rock backed me up until my back was up against a wall, or a

fence, or something. My brain wasn't working enough to know for certain. Nope. All I knew was that my nipples had become sharp peaks poking the fabric out on my tight vest top, my breathing had become laboured, and I was wet. Really fucking wet. Goosebumps erupted all over my arms and I gasped when Rock's mouth collided with my neck.

He trailed kisses up and down my neck, interspersed with little bites, and I shivered with excitement. *Arianna,* I told myself, *stop this foolish shit right now.*

But I didn't.

Fuck, I was pretty sure I *couldn't.*

Like he knew the battle going on in my head, Rock pressed himself flush against me and put his arms on either side of my head, caging me in.

'Are you sure about this?' he asked, his voice rough. 'Because after you agree, I won't stop. It's me and you.'

He cupped my breast with one hand, leaving the other by my head, and I blinked up at him, already close to seeing stars. A tiny moan escaped my parted lips, barely audible over the sound of the rides and screams in the near distance.

I knew I should tell him no. Should say I wasn't sure and that I needed to go back to the tents, or to Tyler, pronto. I opened my mouth to say those exact words.

'I'm sure,' I whispered, saying the exact opposite of what I was going to say.

Shit Ari.

'Good. So am I.'

'We don't have long,' he told me, his tone giving away the thrill he was experiencing at the two of us sharing a secret. An illicit meeting of sorts.

His hands moved from my front to the zipper of his jeans.

Rock pushed the skirt I was wearing up above my hips in one violent motion and I gasped as the cool evening air hit my bare skin. Every touch, every action, was something I'd regret in the morning, I had no doubt, but in the moment, I just wanted *more.*

He moved my underwear to the side, and before I could take a deep breath, he thrust his finger inside me.

'Fuck.' My moan only made him more determined. He added another digit, then a third. 'Fuck!'

He put his other hand over my mouth, cutting off my moans. 'Do you *want* somebody to find us?'

I shook my head. It would probably be a good idea if somebody did find us though, just so things would stop.

I went into my own space mentally, the lights and the music of the festival very much in the background. Rock's fingers disappeared and I felt empty, but within a moment, his dick had replaced them and everything felt right again. Even though I knew it was oh-so-fucking-wrong.

I'm a horrible person.

Yet I still didn't stop. Neither did he.

Our eyes locked and I grunted, the sound incoherent, as his eyes pierced into my soul. My being.

He began to thrust, slowly at first, but then he moved at full speed and that was when we both lost the small thread of control that remained. We got lost in the moment together, the speed of our breathing increasing with each thrust, and it was completely different to our one time the year before.

And the location wasn't the only thing that had changed.

The way he stretched me, the way he moved, all of it felt different.

And oh-so-fucking-good.

Our pleasure hit a crescendo, and the two of us went over the edge at the same time, his cum filling me as we both groaned. 'Fuck.'

I wasn't sure if it was seconds, or minutes, or what, but eventually the two of us untangled from other the other and looked deep into each other's eyes.

I stayed still while Rock righted his clothing, my skirt having fallen back into place once he'd moved. Neither of us spoke for a while.

And then I opened my mouth. 'That was… well, that was something.'

He stayed quiet, rubbing his jaw with agitation, and it was the first action of his that made me realise maybe we weren't on the same page. *Again.*

'Are you going to end things with Savannah?' I asked, my voice barely a whisper.

'Why would I do that?'

'Because you just cheated on her,' I pointed out. 'And maybe we could, I don't know… see how things go.'

'I'm not prepared to do that.'

'Prepared to do *what*?'

'To end my relationship because you've decided we could finally make a go of things together.' He scoffed, a scornful laugh bubbling out. 'Sorry, ice queen, but you don't get to just make the rules up when you feel like it. That's not how life works.'

'But—'

'But nothing.' He laughed again, and my fist clenched at my side. If he kept going, I was going to punch him. 'You don't get to just decide and have me blindly follow you.'

Tears filled my eyes, yet no words left my mouth. For once, I had nothing to say. No comeback or retort to shove in his face.

After one last glance at my face, he walked away, leaving me standing in the darkness all alone. My head couldn't process what the fuck just happened. How had I ended up pressed up against a wall, Rock's dick buried inside me, in the first place? How had I allowed myself to get in such a messy position without even thinking it through?

Fuck hormones and the way they took over.

I moved back into the light and resumed my position in front of the waltzers, lost in thought.

Rock rejected me.

I'd spent so long doing the rejecting that I suppose it hadn't occurred to me he could do the same back.

And fuck did it hurt.

TWELVE
ROCK

age 17, september

FOR THE REST of the festival, I barely saw Arianna—and when I did, she wasn't alone.

Tyler was her shadow, and if it wasn't him beside her, it was Grayson.

As if both of them were making sure I didn't do anything foolish like fuck up my relationship with my girlfriend and piss off my sister all in the space of one weekend. Little did they know, I already had.

Or maybe they *did* know and that was why they weren't letting Ari leave their sight.

I was a fool. I should never have ditched her after having sex with her, and I should never have tried to get her back for what happened the year before in the first place. It was spiteful and cruel—two words I'd never used to describe myself.

I'd just wanted her to feel the way I felt.

My mind wandered back to the events of last year and how I'd ended up with said girlfriend in the first place.

The day after Arianna pushed me away, I drank more than I'd ever drunk before. Every bottle of booze I could get my hands on, I chugged, not caring what was inside.

'You should probably slow down,' Ace said, coming to sit next to

me at the tents. Everybody else was off getting food or heading over to the main stage to watch some of the local bands playing. 'Otherwise, you won't see Dagger play tonight.'

Dagger was the rock band Spencer's parents had somehow managed to pull for the festival this year. They were a huge name and a huge crowd draw, so I knew it was going to get pretty hectic over by the stage.

'I'm not that fussed about seeing Dagger play.' I shrugged, then took another swig of… something that tasted similar to fruit punch? Who the fuck knew, but I was enjoying it anyway. 'The crowd will be hideous.'

'We get to go into the VIP area, remember? Backstage too.'

I had forgotten, but it still didn't overly appeal to me. I'd come to the festival mainly to support Spencer and his family, but also to hang out with my friends. Large crowds weren't something I threw myself into with gusto, which was why I was the only one still sitting at the tents—well, aside from Ace.

'Maybe,' I mumbled. 'Will have to see how the night goes.'

'Well, I'm gonna be there no matter what. Have you seen videos of Banks playing the guitar? Jesus, the man's a legend in the making.'

I shrugged again, his words not having the desired effect.

'Happy for Banks.'

Ace shook his head and stood, rubbing his hands on his jeans. 'Well, I'm gonna leave you here. Clearly, you want to sit and wallow in your misery.'

I waved him off, not even giving him a verbal response. Fuck him. Fuck them all. There was nothing that was going to brighten my day. Not unless Ari came over and told me she took back everything she said last night after we'd shared the most intimate thing a couple could share.

Time passed.

Yet I stayed seated at the tents alone.

The only reason I knew time passed was because the sky was slowly changing from a bright summer's day to a late summer's evening. All pink sky and fluffy clouds.

'Hey!' a voice called out. 'Are you okay?'

I looked up to find a blonde-haired goddess staring at me, the setting sun behind her giving her a glow, her foot tapping on the floor in a way a certain someone I knew had a habit of doing. It made me smile for the first time since I woke up that morning.

'I'm…' I went to say okay, then realised it would be a big fucking fat lie, and I didn't want to lie to the girl on the first meeting. 'Drinking.'

'Do you want to drink alone?' she asked, raising a bottle hidden behind her back, a smile growing wider on her face.

'Are you asking to join me?'

'Yeah. I am.' She laughed, and it hit me deep within. The fact she was being so forthright was a turn-on and I instantly wanted to get to know her better.

'Then come join me,' I said, sweeping my arm out to the empty spot on the floor beside me. 'It's always better drinking together than alone.'

'I'm Savannah, by the way,' she said, taking the spot I'd pointed at. 'Savannah Rhodes.'

'I'm Rock,' I said, reaching out my hand to shake hers. 'Rock Hollowdale.'

'Like the school?'

I nodded. Everybody was surprised when I changed my name to Hollowdale, but it was because it meant so much to my mum that I couldn't say no. 'My stepdad owns the school and I suppose half of the town. Do you go to Hollowdale? I've never seen you around.'

'Not yet. I'm starting this week.'

'That would be why I've never seen you around, then, wouldn't it?'

'Yep. My family just moved to Beurre at the start of the summer.'

'Cool.'

We went silent, both taking small swigs of our drinks, enjoying the peace of the near-empty campsite.

'Surprised you're not over by the main stage,' I said, starting up the conversation again before it became an awkward silence. 'You not a fan of Dagger?'

'I was heading over there when I saw you sitting alone and I couldn't stop myself from saying hey.'

'Don't you want to go and grab a good spot?'

'I'd rather sit here and get to know you.'

And we did just that. Talking about everything and nothing, the alcohol loosening up our lips in more ways than one.

By the time the group came back, we were both quite drunk.

'Dagger was insane!' Tyler said, making his way into the centre of our tent circle. 'You shoulda been there, dude!' Then he spotted Savannah and paused. 'You both should've? Who are you?'

'This is my new girlfriend,' I announced, the words leaving my mouth without me thinking it through. The hours of drinking anything I could get my hands on were coming in hard on my mental faculties clearly.

Obviously, I was lying. I hadn't asked her to be my girlfriend, and I wasn't even sure she was gonna take the bait or call me out in front of everyone, but she did neither of those things.

'I'm Savannah Rhodes,' she said. 'And you must be… Tyler, right?'

He nodded, and I had to admit it impressed me she'd listened to me enough to pick out who was who in my group of friends.

Ari came into my eye line and I sucked in a breath, not having seen her since I left her alone and naked in the tent that morning. My insides went ice-cold. She'd made me so happy and then crushed me mere hours later. She was a stone-cold bitch. The ice queen I'd always said she was.

She also looked like one, her narrowed gaze on the two of us, a shadow of disgust appearing on her face before she could wipe it away.

The booze running through me stopped me from feeling any guilt.

'Hope you two had enough fun that it was worth missing Dagger.' Tyler's face scrunched up, as if he didn't believe anything would've been worth that. But then again, the guy loved rock 'n' roll, so to him, missing Dagger was close to blasphemy in his eyes.

'We did,' I said, making sure our hands locked together were visible to everyone. 'It was more than worth it.'

Nobody said anything, but I noticed a few funny glances from Gray and Tyler.

Well, fuck them! Bet little Miss Ari hadn't told them the truth and just made herself look good instead.

Once the group went off to grab some food or went into their tents for alcohol, Savannah whispered to me out of the corner of her mouth, not wanting to be overheard.

'Why did you tell everyone I'm your girlfriend?'

I shrugged, not having a good answer. 'Would you like to be?'

'I barely know you.'

'You barely know anyone here,' I pointed out. 'And wouldn't it be handy to start school knowing a group of people already?'

'Are you being serious?'

'Deadly.'

'Then sure,' she said with a chuckle. 'I'll be your girlfriend until you come to your senses.'

'Sounds good to me!'

That was a year ago, and neither of us had called it off since. I was pretty sure she'd tell me the next morning to jog on, but she didn't. And the more time I spent with her, the more I realised I liked her. Genuinely.

Maybe not as much as I liked somebody else, but the more time that passed, the easier it was to tell myself lies.

'You okay, Boo?' Savannah came and put her arms around me, her bright eyes looking at me the same way they did that night. 'You look sad.'

'I'm okay,' I replied, pulling her closer. 'Just ready to head home.'

Everyone was packing up their tents, and a sense of sadness that only the end of summer could bring us swept across us all.

'Won't be long now.' She placed a kiss on my cheek. 'Then we can go home and relax before school starts.'

'Want to stay at my place tonight?' I squeezed her waist, not wanting things to change between us, but somehow feeling as though something had. Being back at the festival had brought all the memories tumbling back, and if I was being honest with myself—something I tried to do very little of—I saw my actions in a different light. I saw them how Arianna did the day after we'd slept together for the first, and only, time.

I was the cold-hearted one. I was the prick.

And nothing I did now would erase that.

Thirteen

Arianna

age 17, september

School fucking sucked.

The only saving grace? It was the last year of it.

'Why the long face, Ree?' Gray asked, swaggering over to where I was standing, an energy drink gripped firmly in his hand. God forbid the boy drink water at nine in the morning. 'Something on your mind?'

I slammed my locker door shut and turned to face him fully, the smirk on his lips one I wanted to wipe off with a sharp slap.

'Why are you so annoying?'

'It's a talent of mine,' he replied with a shrug. He waved at a couple of kids who walked past, a shit-eating grin now visible. 'I can tell something's eating at you, so come on, spit it out.'

'Nothing's *eating at me*,' I stressed, wanting him to quit asking questions I didn't want to answer. Because Gray had a knack for pestering me to the point of submission, needling me until nothing but the truth bubbled up and over. 'I just don't wanna be here. That's not a crime, is it?'

'No...' Gray rubbed my shoulder and I flinched at the contact. 'But you've never hated school *this* much, so something musta changed?'

I opened my mouth to answer him, but then a sound carried down the hallway that answered his question for me.

Fuck. My. Life.

Somewhere a little down the hall, Rock was standing with Savannah, who was throwing her head back in laughter at something he'd said, and a chill ran down my spine.

Nobody else was paying attention to Savannah's laughter or the way Rock's hand was resting on the top of her arm. Students were milling around, slamming locker doors or meandering their way down the corridor in order to reach their next class. Friends who hadn't seen each other all summer were catching up, talking a mile a minute, all smiles and joy.

It made me sick.

'Ahhhh,' Gray said, looking in the same direction as me. '*That's* what's eating at you.'

'Her laugh irritates my soul,' I grumbled, bringing the strap of my shoulder bag further onto my shoulder. 'All summer I've had to listen to it, both at the house and at the field. There's no way to escape it! I thought maybe I would here but… clearly not.'

'Her laugh isn't *that* bad,' Gray said, amused by my ire. Then Savannah laughed again. 'I take it back. Her laugh grates on me.'

I chuckled at Gray's all-over faux shiver, glad to have a best friend who was on my side no matter what happened in life.

'You're such a dork.'

'And *you*, my gorgeous best friend, are the light of my life.'

A blush crept up my neck, slowly bleeding across my face, and I smiled—a real, genuine one I couldn't hold back. Gray could say the sweetest things, even if they were disguised as a joke half of the time. My hand punched out, catching him on the shoulder, and he jutted back, rubbing where I hit him.

'That's what I get for saying something nice,' he grumbled, but there was no anger in it.

'Let's go to class, knobhead, before Rock and Savannah decide to grace us with their presence.'

'You're going to have to be around them, Ree. Not like we can escape it.'

'Believe me,' I grunted, heading in the direction of my first class of the day, 'I'm fully aware I cannot escape them.'

Savannah's laughter followed us down the hall.

FOURTEEN
ROCK

age 17, september

HER LAUGHTER TRAVELLED across the field.

Even after all this time, it still did things to my insides to hear her so happy. Even if her amusement had nothing to do with me.

Arianna was standing with Gray and Tyler, laughing about some shit I wasn't a part of, and I gripped my arms around Savannah tighter. My girl was smiling at the girl standing in front of her, and I tuned back into the conversation going on around me.

'Are you going to try out?' Lisa asked, and I supposed she was asking about the dance team tryouts that were coming up.

'Why would I do that?' Savannah asked, leaning back into my chest. 'Being told what to do and where to go by *Remi Riley*? No, thanks.'

'She can't be that bad.' Lisa shook her head. 'She's the year below us, for starters. How can someone be that evil so young?'

'Oh, trust me. The girl's a grade-A bitch. Always has been.'

'Always?'

'Always,' I stressed. 'You don't wanna be friends with that one, or on her team, if you can help it.'

Savannah gave me a warm smile, probably thrilled I'd backed her up.

'I'm gonna try out, but I'll be careful!' Lisa finished her drink, then headed off in the direction of the drinks bucket, leaving me and Savannah alone.

Wonderful.

'How are you?' she asked, turning in my arms to pull me into a tight hug. 'You seem quiet.'

'I'm okay,' I replied, making sure to look at her and not seek out Arianna. 'Just bored of this shit.'

'Bored of the field?'

I gulped down my initial reaction. It made me sound like a right wanker, but when I told her I was "bored of this shit", what I really meant was "I'm bored of playing pretend", specifically with her.

And maybe it would be better if I told her the truth. If I nipped it all in the bud before her feelings for me ran deeper than I suspected they already did. But I was a prick—a self-serving prick—and I couldn't bring myself to end it.

Call me whatever you want, but I didn't want to be at home alone with Ari down the hall.

Nothing would stop me from telling her I didn't care what other people thought. That I wanted to be with her no matter the repercussions.

'Yeah, bored of the field. Just the same old every Friday night, isn't it? Nothing new. Nothing changing. The same people and the same drama.'

'So why don't we bail next week?'

'Bail on the field?' I frowned down at her. 'Bit drastic, babe.'

'But you just said—'

'Yeah, but I didn't mean not show up. Not like we've got anything better to do, is it?'

'We could do each other…' She waggled her eyebrows, and I couldn't help but stare.

Is she trying to be seductive?

'We could…'

'Your parents are never home, and you have such a big empty house… Maybe one Friday soon we can go there instead?'

She's being serious?

'But what about Ari? Our rooms share a wall.' *And a bathroom.*

'She's rarely home, either. Think I've bumped into her like once?' She laughed. 'That was awkward as fuck.'

It was the first I was hearing about it.

'What happened?'

'I was about to use the bathroom at like four in the morning or something, wearing only my knickers and your T-shirt, and I bumped into Arianna standing at her sink looking a little worse for wear.'

'She never mentioned it.'

'Why would she? It was embarrassing for both of us! Neither of us knew what to say, as it was pretty clear what we'd been doing in your room before she got home and I don't have the kind of friendship with her where I can talk to her about sex and stuff.'

'Please don't talk about sex with my sister.'

My sister? Jesus, Rock. Put yourself in between a rock and a hard place, why don't you.

Savannah didn't seem fazed by my tone, cackling away like I'd said something hilarious. 'What? Worried I'm gonna talk about your technique with her? Tell her you're the best lay I've ever had?'

'I thought I was the only lay you've ever had?'

'Semantics, Boo.' She hit my shoulder, her laughter matching that of a villain in a Christmas panto. 'She doesn't know that.'

'And she shall never know that,' I stressed. 'Please don't talk to Ari about any of it.'

'Chill, Boo. I'd never tell her anything intimate like that about us! Wouldn't want to traumatise the girl by telling her about her brother's cock.'

I'd taken a sip of my drink at the *wrong* time, meaning the moment the words left Sav's lips. I choked on the liquid as it went down my throat, causing me to splutter and cough like a fool.

Not that I'd announce it to the world, but Arianna didn't need to be told about my cock because she'd seen it on more than one occasion. The cock in question twitched in my boxers, his thoughts clearly heading in the same direction as mine—imagining Arianna's perfect plump pouting lips wrapped around its head, sucking it like it was her favourite lollipop.

'Yeah, best you don't do that,' I said once the coughing had subsided. The group of people clustered closest to us had looked over during my bout of coughing, but nobody had come over to check if I was okay. Fucking bastards.

I caught Gray's eye and he quirked an eyebrow at me, but I shook my head, not needing him to come over and join the fray. As far as I was aware, he was one of the only people who knew about Ari's and my brief dalliance. *Dalliance? Fucking hell.* I needed a new set of vocabulary, and stat.

'Well, if you want to skip next Friday, I'm game,' she said, bringing the conversation back around to where it started. 'Frankly, your friends bore me.'

'And yours are stellar?'

'Least they do other things than drinking and hooking up with a different person each week.'

'Lisa's draped all over Ace right this moment'—I pointed over to where the two of them were sitting on an ice cooler, somehow balanced while sucking each other's faces—'and I'm pretty sure it was Spencer last week.'

I'd got her there and she knew it, if the small wrinkle in between her eyebrows was anything to go by. It always formed into an M shape when she was thinking about something extra hard, or angry at being proved wrong. One or the other.

'Okay… Everyone *other* than Lisa,' she agreed. We both broke out into laughter, knowing she was right. Lisa really was another breed when it came to not wanting to be tied down—which was totally cool. After all, wasn't that the whole point of being a teenager? Living the way you wanted and learning along the way, all while making stupid fucking decisions that looked good in the dark but never better in the light.

'I'm sorry I said your friends are boring.'

'And I'm sorry I said yours aren't stellar. They're all right, for the most part.'

'And yours are… interesting.'

I laughed again, a full-belly laugh, caught off guard by the way Savannah was trying to save herself but doing a piss-poor job of it. The girl had very little tact when it came to things like that.

'We can agree to disagree,' I told her, pulling her close for a hug. 'Not like we're dating each other's friends.'

'True.' She kissed my cheek, then my lips. A gentle brush of her lips that made me want more as her coconut-scented shampoo twisted its way into my nose. 'We're dating each other, and I don't want that to change.'

'Me neither,' I replied, hoping she didn't hear me waver.

FIFTEEN
ROCK

age 18, october

My eighteenth birthday passed without much fanfare, and honestly, I didn't really mind.

I'd never cared much about going all out on my birthday, mainly because when I was younger, my mum could barely afford to get me any gifts, often spending the remaining pennies of her paycheck on a small cupcake and number candle so she could sing Happy Birthday to me.

Savannah made me feel special enough, and that was all that mattered. Plus, I'd also woken to a cooked breakfast by Arianna filled with all my favourites, plus a bottle of whiskey that must've cost her a fair bob.

That was a month ago, and now we were nearing Arianna's eighteenth birthday, but every time I mentioned it to her, she shrugged it off, which was ridiculous because if anyone knew how much her birthday meant to her, it was me.

'Dude,' Ty said, coming up to where I was standing by my locker in the school hallway. 'Got a favour to ask.'

'Shoot.'

'Reckon we could throw Arianna's cinema and chill party at yours?'

'Where else are you gonna throw it if I say no?'

He paused, rubbing his chin in thought. Wanker probably hadn't even thought of a backup plan and just assumed I'd say yes. Which I was going to do, but still. And even if I said no, Arianna could override me anyway, seeing as it was her house and her birthday.

'Well, we'd get a projector and screen and put it up over at the field, I suppose.' He shrugged, the plan forming in front of his eyes. 'But it's November, and that shit's cold. Guess we could have a bonfire, though…'

'It's fine, dude. We can just do it at my place. Why didn't you ask Ari if it was okay?'

'I wanted it all sorted and in place first. You know what she's like. She wants us to make a big fuss of her, but she'll pretend she doesn't. If I asked her, she'd tell me not to bother.' We both rolled our eyes in sync, knowing he spoke true. I may love the girl, but she was a pain in the arse most of the time.

Shit. Did I just use the word love when thinking of her?

'… invite Savannah if you want.'

'Huh?' I asked, shaking myself mentally so I stopped thinking about whether I loved Ari or not. Not even that, though, because of course I loved her as a friend / family member. But the way I'd thought it, there was nothing family-like in that.

'You can invite Savannah to come if you want to. Otherwise, it'll just be us guys and princess.'

'I'll see what she says, but knowing Ari, she won't want her there.'

'Narh,' he said, not sounding genuine in the slightest. 'She's got nothing against her.'

'No need to lie to me, mate. She thinks she's dim.'

'I shall neither confirm nor deny,' Tyler said, ever the diplomat. 'But if you invite her, Ari isn't going to say anything.'

'We shall see.' I changed the subject, no longer wanting to talk about Savannah. 'What exactly does a cinema and chill party entail, anyway?'

'What it says on the tin. We watch a film and we chill. Me and Gray are going to sort the food and drinks out, so there's no need for you to do anything.'

'Sounds like you've got it all sorted.' *Good for him.* It pissed me off that I wasn't able to throw a party for her birthday and make her feel special the way I wished I could.

And why couldn't I? Because she'd made it perfectly evident multiple times that she wouldn't appreciate it from me. That she wanted our relationship to stay as it was before the night that changed everything for us.

'Only the best for princess on her birthday, right?' He smiled, and for the first time, I wanted to punch that stupid shitting smirk off his face. Everything between him and Ari seemed so easy, so effortless, when everything between me and her was a battle.

'Right,' I agreed. 'Anything you need me to do?'

'Nope, don't think so.' He looked down the corridor and his face lit up when he locked eyes with whoever was heading our way. Oh, who the fuck was I kidding? It could only be one person heading towards us.

'What are you two whispering about over here?' Ari asked, stopping to stand beside Tyler.

'Nothing important, princess,' Tyler replied before I could say anything. 'You know how boring this fucker can be.'

Her face soured when he referenced me. 'You don't need to tell me that.'

'Charming,' I said, meeting her tone. 'You really are an ice queen.'

'I'd rather be an ice queen than a block of stupid.'

'Wow.' I put my palms on my cheeks, feigning shock. 'A block of stupid… What a wonderful insult.'

'Oh, whatever,' she said, a crack in her armour finally showing as her lips tilted up into the slightest of smiles. She turned to face Ty. 'You ready to go?'

'Yeah, just need to go to my locker first.' He smiled at her, his eyes alight with joy.

'Where are you two off to?'

'I promised princess I'd take her out for buffet and mini golf if she beat me in our history dates quiz.'

'But you're terrible at remembering dates,' I pointed out.

'I am. Which is why I'm taking Ari out for a buffet and mini golf.'

We all laughed, but only two of the three of us meant it.

'Have fun,' I said half-heartedly.

'You got any plans?' Ari asked, twirling a strand of her hair around her finger, the nervous energy exuding from her making me uncomfortable.

'Just hanging out with Savannah. Nothing major.'

'You want to join us?' Tyler asked, and I saw Ari wince, which only made me want to say yes.

'Are you sure the two of you won't mind?'

'Ari?' Ty asked. Her eyes said she minded loads, and so did her gritted teeth, but I suppose Tyler was trying to prove that Ari didn't hate Savannah or something.

'Sure,' she bit out.

'Meet at mini golf at six?' Tyler smiled at me, and I knew the bastard was enjoying himself, which meant I couldn't back down.

I smiled back. 'Meet you there.'

SAVANNAH WASN'T OVERLY THRILLED when I told her our plans for the evening—or at least when I told her the plans included Ari and Tyler too—but she was putting her game face on regardless.

'Have you ever been to this mini golf before?' I asked her as we made our way from my car to the entrance. It was a relatively new one in the town next to ours, attached to Lakeland Lanes bowling alley, and was completely indoors.

I'd been once before with the guys and won, so I was feeling super confident going in that I'd beat them all.

'I'm not exactly a huge fan of mini golf,' she said, placing her hand on mine. 'Never been very good at it, honestly, and the themes are always so tacky. Pirates or dinosaurs or something equally naff.'

'Naff?' I scoffed. 'What's naff about dinosaurs or pirates?'

'Everything.'

'Well, lucky for you, this mini golf isn't themed to either dinosaurs or pirates.'

'What theme does it have?' she asked warily, and I couldn't blame her. Pirates and dinosaurs may be tacky in her eyes, but usually if places went outside those two themes, they were even worse. 'Or fuck, is it one of those places that think it's above a theme and doesn't have one at all?'

The horror in her tone caught me and a laugh came from deep within. 'Well… each hole has its own theme.'

'Wonderful,' she muttered but shut up when we bumped into Tyler and Ari. Quite literally. We weren't watching where we were going and went straight into their backs. 'Oh, hey, guys.'

'Hey,' Tyler replied once he and Ari got their balance back. 'You ready to get whipped?'

'I beat you last time. Plus, we both know you can't handle the pressure after a few holes.'

'There is so much I want to say to that,' Ari said with a giggle that knocked me back. 'But I won't because there's a lady present.'

'You not including yourself in that, princess?'

'Fuck no,' she blurted. Nobody pointed out that if Ari felt that strongly about not being classed as a lady, then maybe what she'd said was an insult. Knowing Ari, she'd known it was an insult and said it anyway, hoping Savannah wasn't bright enough to figure it out.

'Let's go!' Tyler said, drawing the attention. 'I'm feeling lucky.'

The four of us made our way inside the air-conditioned building and went upstairs to the entrance, an underlying buzz that could be considered just friendly competition but was most likely dislike brewing in the air.

Once we'd paid for twenty holes, ten per course, and grabbed our clubs and balls, we went through the barn door that led to the first hole.

From the moment the four of us were in the confined space, I regretted agreeing to come. The only reason I'd said yes was because I knew it would piss off Ari if we crashed her night, but I hadn't actually thought through how Sav and I would feel.

The walls were close to the green, and there was barely any space to manoeuvre, let alone swing a golf club. I was a big guy and tight spaces weren't my friend.

'Isn't this cosy?' Tyler said, filling out the scorecard. 'Right, Savannah's up first, then me, followed by Ari and Rock.'

'Why'd you choose that order?' Sav asked, looking at me for guidance I couldn't give. Was Tyler picking on her by having her go first? I doubted it, but I also wouldn't put it past him to do something like that if it made Ari smile.

'Because our initials spell STAR, see?' he said, showing Ari the scorecard, and she rolled her eyes, a smile playing on her full lips. 'And stars are fun.'

'Stars are fun?' Ari repeated, but in a playful way. 'Can you hear yourself sometimes?'

'I can always hear myself,' Tyler said with a nod as if that ended that. 'Right, come on, Savannah. Step right up!'

'Just a heads-up,' Sav said, walking over to the start. 'I'm not very good, so don't be expecting any hole-in-ones or anything.'

'Pretty sure it's impossible to get a hole-in-one on this course, babe,' I said, trying to make her feel better. It was known for being notoriously difficult. There was barely any space to swing, but they somehow expected you to swing with enough power to get your ball up a four-foot half pipe. There was even one hole in the dark, the only light coming from badly painted UV squiggles, where you needed to get your ball to the top of a large pinball machine so it could exit the hole that led to the rest of the green, and not the hole at the bottom that fed it back to you.

'Yeah, no pressure!' Ari joined in, and I smiled, thrilled she was trying to make Savannah feel a little more welcome. It was all my fault for putting her in the situation in the first place just to satisfy an itch I was having to ruin Ty and Ari's time together.

Shit. Am I a date crasher? Is this a date for them? My anger at the thought pissed me off. I was one of the biggest hypocrites when it came to that.

When Sav finished the hole in five, Tyler took his turn, then Arianna, and everything was going swimmingly for at least the first five holes.

Then the cracks started to show.

'Can you not step on my foot,' Ari hissed in my ear, or at least in the direction of my ear, seeing as she was at least five inches shorter than me.

'Please give me some space!' Savannah shouted when it was her turn on the pinball machine hole. She'd already hit her ball twenty times, but nobody wanted to point out that maybe she should just place her ball on the other side—none of us would penalise her for it. 'I can't breathe with you hovering over me!'

'There's not exactly space for us all.' Tyler laughed, unfazed by her. 'We're doing the best with what we have.'

'Eurgh!' Savannah stomped her feet, her anger rising. 'Why won't this stupid ball just land in the stupid hole!' She stomped her foot again, and in slow motion I watched as her club left her manicured grip, hurtled through the small space, and landed directly in Arianna's face.

'Fuck!' she shouted as the club collided with her nose. 'Fuck!'

Without thinking, I went straight over to her, grabbed her chin to keep her still, and assessed the damage. Blood was trickling from her nose, seconds before it turned into a downpour, and my gut reaction was to use the bottom of my T-shirt to staunch the flow, which meant I was unable to leave her side to go ask Savannah if she was okay.

Rookie boyfriend move.

'I think that's enough mini golf fun for you!' Tyler told Ari, rubbing her arm in a way I wished I could comfort her but knew I couldn't. 'Think it's time for us two to head over to Heanue's.'

Heanue's was the world buffet across the parking lot, and even though it wasn't always the best, it hit the spot like no other buffet I'd ever experienced. It was one of Ari's favourite guilty pleasures—no wonder Ty was taking her there.

'Let me,' Tyler said to me, moving my T-shirt away from Ari's nose and replacing it with his own. 'Come on, princess. Can't give Savannah another chance to club you, can we?'

It was that moment when I should've stuck up for Sav. Should've said she didn't do any of it on purpose, or something to that effect, but I didn't. I stayed silent, feeling like a spare part now that I wasn't the one comforting Ari.

'You two can continue if you want,' Ty said, handing me the scorecard and the little pencil that came with it. 'We'll meet you at Heanue's.'

'No, it's fine,' Savannah said, speaking for the first time since she hit Ari. 'I don't feel much like a world buffet right now. You two go and have fun without us. I really am so very sorry, Arianna.'

'Thab's otay,' Ari replied, her words muffled through Tyler's top.

Ty laughed. 'Not like you did it on purpose, right?'

A chill covered the space and nobody said anything more. I knew Savannah hadn't done it on purpose, but I also felt partially responsible nonetheless. It was because of me and my dickheadedness that she was even put in a scenario where she could physically maim somebody.

'We'll see you guys back at yours,' Ty said, ushering Ari

away, who gave a small wave before they disappeared out of sight.

'What the fuck was that about?' Sav turned to me, steel in her voice, ice in her eyes. 'You didn't even check if I was okay!'

'You weren't the one hit in the face by flying metal!' I turned to face her fully. 'Or the one bleeding. You didn't need me to check on you.'

'But I did.' She stomped her foot again as her bottom lip wobbled. 'I threw a temper tantrum in front of your friend, then made your sister bleed! They'll never like me now.'

'They already like you.'

'No, they don't,' she said, her tone flat, and I thought it would be insulting if I reiterated my lie. Not that it was a complete lie. They liked her, a little—just not loads. It had never bothered me much before because they weren't the ones dating her, so what did it matter, but before the evening went to shit, I realised it was kind of fun to have a partner included in group things. 'They tolerate me.'

'Well, then it's a good thing *I* like you, isn't it?' I walked closer, placing my club down and putting the scorecard and pencil in my jeans pocket before taking her in my arms. 'Who cares what anyone else thinks.'

'Can we just go home? I really fucking hate mini golf.'

'Sure,' I said, not wanting to push her further. 'We can order in and have our own world buffet.'

'Okay.' Her voice was small and timid, and it was the first time in a while I wanted to do nothing else but make her happy. She seemed so petite, so fragile, that I felt the urge to take her and keep her safe from everyone—including from me.

And that was how I knew I was one of the worst pricks alive.

Sixteen

Arianna

age 17, november

It was Tyler who had suggested we all celebrate my eighteenth birthday together.

So, it was Tyler I wanted to murder when all of us were spread out across the cinema room to celebrate.

The usual suspects were there, of course. Gray, Spencer, and Ace had all shown up with various gifts and they all seemed a little *too* eager for me to open them. Tyler of course was there, having arranged the entire thing, and had helped me set up all the food and drink he'd ordered in for us all.

Then there was Rock, who I knew would show up because a) he was invited and b) because it was his house too. What I hadn't expected was for him to show up with Savannah fused to his side, her arm tight around his waist and his draped on her shoulder, pulling her tight.

Ever since the whole nearly taking off my nose at the mini golf course thing, I'd avoided them even more than before. Had the girl hurt me on purpose? No, of course not, *but* I'd had a bruise for a week that wasn't fading fast enough for my liking.

Savannah's gaggle of friends were also with them—girls I'd never spoken to before—all laughing and joking about what a fun time we were all gonna have.

Okay…

Tyler's eye caught mine and I raised my eyebrows, questioning if it was his idea for them to come, but his responding frown told me he'd had no clue.

So, it was Rock's idea… Good to know.

Maybe it was because I always grumbled that nobody cared about me or my birthday enough, and he wanted me to feel loved, but how could I feel loved when I'd never even spoken to them? They were here for free food and free booze, simple as.

As usual, my dad was away in the city on business and of course Gigi had gone with him. If there was one thing I knew about my dad, it was that he wasn't like the typical sleazy businessman you heard about. He definitely couldn't have a different girl in every city as his wife never left his side. Maybe that was why she went, to ensure he never strayed, but knowing my dad, he really did love her, so he probably wouldn't anyway.

He had sent a birthday card, though, and ordered my favourite birthday cake to be delivered, so I couldn't be too mad at the man. Our relationship was frosty at best, and if he didn't work so dang hard, I'd never have had the privileged life I did. Swings and roundabouts and all that. And I wasn't going to utter some bullshit about how I'd have preferred his love over the money he provided us with, because yeah, my mental state definitely would've preferred a father's love, but there was no way of knowing for sure how having less money would've affected me. I was handed the lot I was handed, and that was that.

'You got the film picked, ice queen?' Rock called out, grabbing my attention away from the food I was staring at as a distraction, and I looked over to find him on one of the love seats, Savannah on his lap.

'Not just yet,' I admitted. 'But I've got it narrowed down to a top five.'

'Please, Ree, please no *To Kill a Mockingbird*,' Gray pleaded.

'How'd you know it was in my top five?'

'Because it's *always* in your top five,' he whined. 'Actually, scratch that. It's usually in your top two.'

'Can't help that it's a fucking masterpiece.'

'It's in black and white.'

'Nothing wrong with a black-and-white movie,' I pointed out. 'Maybe one day soon you'll appreciate the classics, Grayson!'

He scoffed. 'Doubt it.'

'So, what is this top four then?' Tyler piped up, coming over to stand beside me, reaching out a comforting hand I took with gratitude.

All eyes in the room swivelled to me and I instantly felt self-conscious. Not because of the boys—I'd grown up around them and they all knew my taste in movies—but because of the girls I didn't know, who didn't know me.

'Okay, so obviously *To Kill a Mockingbird* is out,' I said, boring my eyes in Grayson's direction, and everyone chuckled. 'So, we're left with *Pride and Prejudice*, the Kiera Knightley version, of course, *Atonement*, *Hunger Games*, and *Stand By Me*.'

'Ew,' one of Savannah's friends said, loud enough to stop everyone in their tracks. 'Why are all of them boring? And also, I'd like to point out, highly fucking depressing.'

'Sorry?' I sputtered, caught off guard.

'Every one of your options is like based on a book or something,' the girl said, not realising the hole she was digging for herself. 'I thought we were coming here to watch an action movie or something scary and fun.'

'I don't like scary movies,' was all I could think to reply without getting mad. 'And I happen to think adaptations *are* fun.'

'I suppose we all have a different definition of fun,' the girl said.

Who the fuck even is she?

I'd only seen her around a couple of times and I didn't know her name, yet she apparently felt comfortable enough to come to my house, for my birthday, and spurt out her strong opinions without fear.

'It's Ari's birthday, and what she wants is what she gets,' Grayson said, his tone brooking no argument from anybody in the room. 'And if you don't like that, then you can leave. Pretty sure the birthday girl didn't invite you, anyway.'

'Savannah invited me,' she said, not looking in the least ashamed at her actions.

'Last time I checked,' Gray said, his tone getting darker and darker with each word uttered, 'Savannah doesn't have the right to determine who's invited to Ree's birthday, so I suggest you either shut the fuck up or go.'

'Are you gonna let him speak to me like that?' the girl asked, turning to face Savannah, who looked like a rabbit caught in the headlights, her wide eyes telling me she didn't know how to approach the situation. On the one hand, she clearly invited her, so she was responsible for her acting like a bitch, but on the other hand, she wanted to stay on my good side because I was a part of her boyfriend's family.

'Err... I...' She looked around for help, but none was forthcoming. If anything, she ran into averted eyes or disappointed gazes. 'Rock?'

'If I get involved, babe, it won't be on your side,' he grumbled, looking pissed, his eyes narrowed on the bitchy girl. 'So, either deal with this, or you can get out too.'

'What?' she screeched, jumping off his lap to stare at him. 'You'd kick me out, too?'

'Yep, and if you plan to cause even more of a scene, then I'll walk you to the door myself.'

'Boo,' she whined, pouting out her bottom lip. 'What's happening here?'

'What's happening is you invited Maria.'

Ah, that's the girl's name.

'And she's ruining our fun time. If you don't want to watch the film Ari picks, that's fine. No hard feelings. But decide now before it begins 'cause I'm not having you grumble your way through it. You or your friends.'

Watching it unfold was more interesting than a movie, that was for sure, but I wasn't gonna blurt it out loud. Rock's gaze was narrowed on Savannah, and Savannah's bottom lip was beginning to quiver, looking seconds away from crying.

Tyler's hand squeezed mine, and it made me jump. I'd forgotten we were holding hands, but the moment I remembered, it grounded me. Who gave a fuck what *Maria* thought? It was my birthday and yeah, my tastes may not be for everyone, but I wasn't trying to impress everyone. Fuck, I wasn't trying to impress *anyone*.

'Maria, if you don't want to stick around, then that's cool with me. Or any of you girls. I'll meet up with you after.' Savannah gave a small nod to Rock, and it was clear she'd chosen to stay in his good books. If I liked her more, I'd probably warn her about choosing your boyfriend over your friends, but I didn't, so I wouldn't.

'Seriously? I thought we'd be getting our booze on, not our snooze on.' Maria was standing, tapping her toe on the ground, ready to bolt the moment she was able. 'You're gonna stay here, Sav?'

'Yeah?' Savannah said, but it wasn't filled with certainty, her voice rising at the end so it sounded more like a question.

'Suit yourself,' Maria spat. 'Come on, girls!'

The others all stood and followed Maria out of the room, and I gave another glance at Savannah, who was blinking back tears. For some reason, I'd always assumed she was the ringleader of her group, but clearly that wasn't the case. I'd thought they all showed because she'd demanded they show, but maybe she invited them to seem cool?

It made me feel for her—just a little.

Nobody liked being the odd one out, and everybody wanted to feel like they were a part of something. She'd only started at Hollowdale the year before and making new friends in a town where everybody has known each other forever must be difficult.

It was one of the things I loved about being a Rebel. Yeah, the name was bullshit and something we made up as kids that had stuck around like a bad smell, even though it was super rare any of us did anything even remotely rebellious, but it meant I was always included. Always surrounded by people who loved me and cared about me and wanted me to be happy.

And I wanted nothing but the same for them all, too.

Once Maria and the other girls had left, a hush of silence went through the room. Savannah had placed herself back on Rock's lap, like the last ten minutes hadn't happened, sadness still lingering on her features.

'Well, now that drama's been dealt with,' Gray said, looking at me with a wide grin, 'let's pick a film, birthday girl.'

I smiled at him, thrilled about him always having my back, no matter what shit we found ourselves in. 'Thank you.'

'No need to thank me,' he said, his smile somehow widening further. 'You're my girl.'

'Don't make me cry,' I said through a laugh, holding back my tears. 'Now that the drama is done, I think I'm ready to announce my chosen film.'

'And what film's that?' Rock asked, and although he was smiling at me over Savannah's head, his eyes were tense.

'*Stand By Me*, of course.'

The tension in his eyes receded. 'Of course.'

SEVENTEEN
ROCK

age 14, august

AFTER THE WEDDING, my mum and her new husband jetted off rather fast to some exotic honeymoon location and left me and Ari at home. Alone. With no adult supervision.

Ever since the wedding, I couldn't get the thought of Ari in her bridesmaid dress out of my mind. The way her curly bright red hair rested on her bare shoulders, the way her jade green eyes lit up every time somebody said something that slightly amused her.

I shook my head to knock the thought of Ari away.

Most kids my age would take being home alone as the perfect opportunity to throw a party, and it was in my plans to, but not just yet. The house didn't feel like home. Not *my* home.

Mum and I had moved in not long before the wedding, to get our bearings, but there was something about the large, empty mansion that made me uncomfortable. We'd moved from the other side of the divide—the invisible line that runs through the centre of Beurre, dividing those with money from those who don't—into a large mansion in the Hawthorn Hills and I still wasn't used to it yet. Our last place had four rooms altogether: a kitchen, a bathroom, and two bedrooms.

Yet the Hollowdale mansion had more rooms than I knew about—I was still counting.

One room I liked, though, was the kitchen. It was stocked with everything you could dream of. All my favourite meals, snacks, and treats in one place. The housekeeper, a lovely little lady named Mrs Billins, took a shine to me after our first conversation and had done all she could since to keep me happy. Bless her.

'Want to watch a film with me tonight?' Arianna asked, walking into the kitchen and opening one of the large American-style fridge doors to peek inside. She closed the door without grabbing anything and turned to look me in the eye. 'Unless you already have plans?'

'Nope, no plans,' I told her, assessing the situation. Ari and I had known each other for most of our lives. Ever since we were five and Grayson's mum became her dad's housekeeper. Gray and I lived near each other on the Hollowdale estate, plus we were in the same class at school, so we were mates. It was through him I met Ari. Back then, she was a short brunette kid with an attitude, always mouthing off about something. Fighting all the boys, even those bigger than her, if they said something she disagreed with. She hadn't changed much over the years.

Except her hair was now a pillar box red and she was taller—slightly. Oh, and her body was pretty nice to look at. Okay, understatement. Her body was curvy in all the right places, and she was every guy's walking wet dream. Plus, she was one of the most beautiful girls I'd ever seen. You know. Minor things…

And now she was my fucking stepsister. What a cruel joke.

'Thought you'd be hanging with the guys tonight.'

'It's a bit… awkward, to say the least.'

'Because of Maxwell?' She opened the fridge door again and took out a bottle of water. 'Is Spencer okay?'

'I'm not sure, honestly. He won't talk to any of us since Max died. His mum says he doesn't leave his room often, either. Hopefully, after the funeral, he'll open up to us a bit.'

Ari nodded before taking a gulp of her water. I knew she wasn't looking forward to the funeral. Fuck, nobody *looked forward* to funerals, but Ari and Maxwell weren't exactly close when he was alive. He looked down on her, called her pipsqueak, and was always baiting her for being the only girl to hang around with us. But she would go, no matter how much she didn't want to, for Spencer. We'd all go for Spencer.

Towards the end, none of us were really that close with Max, but most of that was because he was three years older than us and hung around with a crowd more interested in girls and booze.

'So, did you want to watch a film with me tonight?' she asked, changing the subject, and the tightness around my chest loosened a little, and then I thought about how we'd both be sitting in close proximity in the dark if we watched a film, and my pulse began to thrum in my throat.

'What film you got in mind?'

'Well, I don't have one in mind. I asked you on the fly,' she said with a small laugh. 'But knowing you, it'll be some action crap.'

'Action crap is the best type of crap, but fine, I'll let you pick.' I knew she'd jump on the chance to choose the film—I also knew she'd pick something I would never want to watch but would watch anyway just because she wanted me to.

'Are you sure that's a good idea?' The smirk on her face worried me, but I stayed firm and gave a nod. 'Cool! Then I choose *Stand by Me*.'

'Again?'

'Again.' Laugh lines formed at the corners of her mouth as she beamed at me, all her perfect, straight teeth on show, and I swallowed a groan. I really needed to get a hold of myself around her. No matter how much I wanted to, I couldn't act on my feelings for her. 'It's my favourite.'

'I don't understand why.'

'I can list five things off the top of my head.'

'And they are?'

'River Phoenix. A young Kiefer Sutherland. The soundtrack. All the quotable lines. And it's an adaptation of a Stephen King novel, which automatically puts it in a higher category.'

'If you say so.'

'I'll meet you in the cinema room in fifteen minutes?' she asked, opening the fridge door once more, but this time grabbing a can of lemonade from inside—must be all out of cream soda, which I knew was her go-to. It grossed me the fuck out, though. I couldn't understand how anybody was able to drink it without the smell putting them off. It was vile.

'See you there.'

I had fifteen minutes to calm the fuck down. I could do that. Right?

THE FILM PLAYED on the large projector screen of the cinema room, and I struggled to keep my eyes open.

A dark room and a bright screen were guaranteed to send me to sleep—especially if the film was one I didn't want to watch in the first place, which seemed to happen to me a lot with Ari around pulling the strings.

What can I say? I'm a sucker for her.

The only thing that was keeping me awake? The giggles coming from Arianna's mouth at certain points during the movie that she found the funniest—so basically the entire damn film.

Every time that giggle left her lips, my dick reacted. I couldn't help it. It was like a drug I couldn't get enough of. Something I wanted to pour directly into my veins and have on tap for eternity.

'If you had the chance to go see a dead body, would you?' Ari asked out of the blue at the exact moment I took a sip from my drink, then proceeded to spray it all over myself.

Her laughter filled the air and she looked at me with a wicked glint in her green eyes.

'You okay there?'

'You caught me off guard.'

'Just answer the question and I promise I won't tell another rebel about this.'

'That's rich,' I scoffed. 'You're gonna text Grayson the moment you look at your phone.'

'Do you have that little faith in me?' Her mouth opened with fake shock. 'I do have a tiny bit of integrity, you know?'

'No,' I said sourly. 'I don't know that. I swear Gray knows a lot more than I've ever told him.'

'I can't help it that the boy's a gossip.' She shrugged, turning back to the screen, ready to press play on the movie I hadn't realised she'd paused. 'He's got a way of making me talk.'

'Sure he has.' I tried not to have sour feelings when I thought of Arianna's friendship with Grayson, but it was hard. The two of them were so carefree together, so in sync and able to be their true selves that I was a tad jealous. Not that I'd admit it to them or anything. 'To answer your poorly-timed question though, no, I don't think I would.'

'Even if it meant the adventure of a lifetime?'

'No dead body is going to lead to the adventure of a lifetime, Ari, that's why this is a film and fictional. Plus, it's a bit grim, isn't it, when you think about it?'

'Stephen King may write grim things, Rock, but the dude's a master at it.'

'If you say so.'

'I do. Ever since I read the one where people literally poo aliens I can only think of the man as a genius.' I raised my eyebrows at her statement but she ignored me, and pressed play, getting comfortable in her chair once more, and instead of looking back at the screen, I found my eyes perusing her, starting at her bright hair that was up in a ponytail, leaving her slender neck in full view. 'Thanks.'

'Thanks?'

'For chilling with me tonight,' she clarified. 'You could've gone out with the guys or whatnot instead of watching a film you don't even like.'

'Couldn't leave my stepsis alone, could I?'

The moment the words left my lips, I cringed, and Ari winced, her eyes still locked on the screen, as if turning to look at me would only make things worse.

Shit.

I'd meant it as some cute, funny line, but all it did was highlight our new situation. Highlight the fact we were now related (loosely) in the eyes of everyone. But the thoughts I had about her were *not* the thoughts you had about your sister—trust me on that.

Double shit.

EIGHTEEN
ROCK

age 18, december

As it did every year, New Year's Eve crept up on us.

And the girl I was facing, the one I would be sharing a midnight kiss with, wasn't the girl I wanted to be facing or sharing a midnight kiss with.

Which made me a massive arsehole because if I'd got my shit into gear, I could've prevented everything from going the way it had, and I only had myself to blame. Like any time that thought came to mind, it didn't sit well in my gut.

'Thank you for inviting me,' Savannah murmured, looking at our surroundings in awe. Somehow, we'd found ourselves up the hill at Hawthorn Academy attending the charity gala they threw each new year. It was *the* event for the rich and wealthy to show off their charity chops, and their families, in an acceptable way.

My mum and Tony were dancing beside us on the dance floor, looking happier than ever, and I smiled. My mum's happiness was the reason I'd made the decisions I had. Her happiness meant a fuck ton more than my own did, that was for sure.

Growing up, we hadn't had much. We'd lived in a small two-bedroom apartment on the Hollowdale Estate, with barely enough money to cover both bills and food. There were weeks when my mum didn't eat more than a can of baked beans because all the money she set aside for food went on food for me.

I could never repay her for what she'd done, choosing my health and happiness over hers every time, and even though that was expected of parents, I'd still heard horror stories where that wasn't the case. So how could I stop her from marrying Tony when she'd given up so much for me? And what would I have even said? *Oh, by the way, Mum. I super fancy the daughter of the dude you wanna marry, so maybe you shouldn't marry him.*

That woulda gone down well. *Not.*

Especially as we were only fourteen at the time.

'Isn't this place so fancy?' Savannah whispered, taking in the dresses and the decor of the hall. 'I can't believe kids go to school here.'

'Can you imagine this being the main hall at Hollowdale?' I chuckled, envisioning the hall at our school and remembering everything lacking in comparison to our current surroundings. 'Just from being here, I feel like we're making the place look dirty.'

'How come you don't go to school here?'

'Because Tony owns Hollowdale High…'

'Oh yeah,' she tittered. 'That makes sense.'

We continued dancing along with the band playing, and I tried to find Arianna in the crowd, but I couldn't see where she'd slipped off to.

'You look amazing,' Sav whispered, drawing my attention once more, taking me in from head to toe. 'You look like you've been around this extravagance your whole life. It's natural for you.'

'Believe me,' I said, my tone gruff, 'none of this comes naturally to me. It's all for my mum.'

'Are you close with your mum? We've nearly been together a year and a half and I don't think I've seen you talk to her more than three times—tonight being one of the three.'

'We used to be super close back when it was just us two, but since she married Tony, I've barely seen her, honestly.' I looked over at my mum, saw her bright smile, and a buzz of warmth filled me. It was her smile that gave me pause anytime I considered throwing caution to the wind and pursuing something with Arianna.

'She seems happy.'

'She is. She's the only reason you'd ever catch me in a suit.' I fidgeted, self-conscious in the grey suit I'd donned for the event. Savannah looked beautiful in a dress Arianna had given her the night before. I was worried when I approached Ari, but I should've known Ari wouldn't mind. Of course she helped Sav when I asked—she wasn't the kind of girl who would make another feel uncomfortable on purpose.

'Well, I'm happy to see you in one. Thank you for inviting me tonight.'

Sometimes, when you didn't know what to say, an action was easier. I leaned closer and placed a gentle kiss on Savannah's cheek, not wanting to ruin the makeup she'd spent hours on.

She really did look beautiful.

And I felt like a prick because even though I was a lucky fucker to be with her, I still couldn't get how beautiful Arianna looked out of my mind, either.

'Who are they?' she asked, nudging her head in the direction of the group now approaching my mum and Tony. 'They seem important.'

'Ah, now the tallest is Edward Hawthorn,' I said, turning us an inch to see the group better. 'He owns this school and anything with the Hawthorn name, so he and Tony have that in common. The woman embracing Mum is his wife, Lottie. Then the other two are Henry Brandon and Baron Henrick.'

'Isn't Henrick the guy with the mansion in the woods?' she whispered, as close to my ear as she could get. 'The one with the dead wives?'

I shrugged, unsure for certain, but just from looking at the dude, I didn't doubt the rumours.

'He's a little creepy.' Savannah shivered, and I didn't blame her. The guy gave me bad vibes.

It was at that moment I spotted Arianna at the edge of the dance floor, talking in depth with Griffin Cooper and Clover Luck—yep, that really was her real name. In previous years, I would hang with Arianna, barely speaking to her, but making the rounds and talking to the people our age who went to school here. Plus, because Tony sometimes did business with their parents, so we knew them enough to pass the time at events.

'Ari seems to be enjoying herself,' Savannah said when she noticed what had gained my attention. 'She looks friendly with those two.'

'We've known them for years,' I said, looking away. 'Bit too rich for my liking, but they're nice enough, I suppose.'

'Just not your type of people.'

'For sure,' I agreed. 'I'd much prefer hanging at the field with the Rebels than being cooped up here, unable to escape.'

'It's been nice to see how the other half lives. I'm not gonna lie. Thank you again.'

'No need to thank me, babe,' I murmured, trying to shake the ominous feeling spreading through my body. 'You're my girl.'

The words were true, but why did they make me feel so awful?

AT A QUARTER TO MIDNIGHT, I excused myself and went in search of the toilets.

Savannah had been her charming self all evening, and I'd barely seen Ari, but something wasn't sitting right with me about any of it. Yet I couldn't put my finger on what it was exactly. Maybe it was the fact I was spending the evening with a great girl, but not *the* girl.

As I exited the bathroom and headed back to the hall, I was walking slower than usual, not in any rush.

'Oi!' a voice hollered, catching my attention. 'Rock!'

I turned to find Griffin Cooper sauntering towards me, Clover still by his side.

'You ditching this shindig too?' he asked, walking over, dragging Clover along with him. He'd always been the kind of guy who got what he wanted—all while keeping a big grin on his face.

'Sadly, no,' I replied, checking the time on my phone. It was five minutes to midnight. I still had time to get back and find Sav for our kiss. 'Heading back in, actually.'

'Unlucky, mate! Clo and I thought we'd sneak out while nobody was looking. See the new year in without any eyes on us, if you know what I mean.' He waggled his eyebrows and I laughed. Clo elbowed him, but there was a smile on her face, so we all knew she wasn't mad at him. He was one of those people it was hard to stay mad at, even if they were a major prick half of the time.

'Well, as fun as this has been,' I said, taking a step away from them, 'enjoy the rest of your night, you two!'

'Oh, we will! Just one thing before you go.'

'Yeah?'

'Why are you here with that other girl? We've had a bet going for ages now about when you and Ari will get over yourselves and fuck.' Clo elbowed him again, harder, and he rubbed at where her elbow had connected with his side. 'What? I lost about two years ago.'

I couldn't help but ask, 'Who's winning?'

'Oliver, of course. That fucker's always right, and for once I hoped you'd come through for me, but nope. Another year and still nothing.'

'Sorry to let you down.'

'Ah, well, it's a new year, after all! Maybe this will be the year.'

I waved goodbye, still chuckling at him, not answering his final sentence. It may be a new year, but I doubted *that* would happen… again.

I could've told him he was closer to winning than he knew, seeing as I'd slept with Arianna fifteen months ago (not that I was counting), but a gentleman didn't hoe and tell.

'Where have you been?' Sav hissed when I made it back to her side with minutes to spare. 'I thought I'd be stood here alone at midnight like Prince Charming!'

'Prince Charming would've been chasing his princess down the steps, actually.'

'Just join in with the countdown and kiss me at the end of it!'

'Aye, aye, captain.'

Lucky for me, she couldn't hear the ire in my voice.

Nineteen

Arianna

age 18, january

'Fuck yes, like that.'

Grayson's moan reached me, and I knew I didn't want to interrupt the moment but had no other choice. The boy was talking about sorting his shit out, then there he was, balls deep in some random girl at the field in view of anyone who went looking for them.

His gaze moved from the girl with her lips around his dick and locked with mine. I probably looked like the angry best friend coming to ruin his fun. I was standing with my arms crossed over my chest, my bright red hair freshly dyed, tied atop my head in a messy bun, and my foot was tapping away in irritation, already having seen enough of this shit show.

'Get over here,' I growled, hoping he wouldn't stick around to finish what he'd started before coming over. He'd done it before, and I never wanted a repeat of that moment. Watching your best friend's face contort in the pleasures of ecstasy just didn't hit the same when you had zero romantic feelings towards said person. It just made you cringe. He rolled his eyes, and I knew he was also debating with himself about whether to wrap it up or keep it out.

'Can I—' he hollered.

Fucking cheek of him.

'Grayson,' I growled again, lower than before. 'I'll come and remove your dick from her mouth myself if you don't wrap it up.'

'Okay, okay,' he said, raising his hands in a gesture of peace before placing them on the shoulders of the girl on her knees. 'Show's over.'

I pretended not to hear the sound of his dick releasing from her vice-like jaw grip, but it was a sound that'd haunt me for years to come. The girl looked up at Grayson, ignoring my presence completely, and batted her eyelashes, as if her wide eyes would get him to forget about me.

'Are you sure you're gonna let little Miss Ari ruin our fun?' she asked, and I scoffed at her audacity, but also sort of admired the tenacity.

'We're done here,' Gray repeated, taking a step back and—FINALLY—putting his dick away. He adjusted himself before walking over to me, which I appreciated, but I was still tapping my foot, pissed as all get-out he even put me in the situation in the first place.

'What did you do that for?' he whined, his eyebrows rising in question.

'What did I do *what* for? Why did I stop you from making *yet another* stupid decision? Oh, I don't know, Grayson. Maybe because you need to sort your fucking shit out and stop getting your dick wet with literally any girl who throws herself at you.'

Okay, so maybe that came out a little bitter and a lot more sour than I intended, but my point was valid. Gray just never knew when to say when. With anything.

'Maybe if you took one of the dicks who throw themselves at you up on their offer, you wouldn't be so uptight?'

'Are you shitting me?' I laughed, but there was no humour in it. 'Are you seriously telling me I need to get laid? Come on, Gray. You're better than that.'

'Am I? Just tell me what you want.'

I wasn't answering his question because I knew he was better than that. He just didn't believe it. Grayson never believed anything good I said about him, so most of the time it wasn't worth the bother. 'We're going.'

I grabbed his arm before he could respond and pulled him towards where I'd left my car parked with the others.

'Like fuck we are.' He dug his heels in and sweat covered my brow at the effort it took to keep him moving.

'Grayson Smith,' I grumbled, pulling out the big guns. 'Do not push me. We're going back to mine now and that is final.'

'Why?' he asked, standing on his tiptoes to look over at the crowd still occupying the field. I didn't follow his gaze, knowing what he would find. 'Oh. You can't stand to watch your step-brother get it on, huh?'

'Shut up,' I said, jostling him to the point he lost his balance and nearly fell, almost taking me down too. 'Are you coming with me or not?'

He blew out a breath, dragging out his charade. We both knew he was going to leave with me. He always did.

'I'll come,' he said, looking into my eyes until I got uncomfortable and had to look away from his scrutiny. 'But you need to tell me what's going on with you and Rock.'

'Nothing's going on,' I murmured.

'You may fool everybody else, but you'll never fool me, *pipsqueak.*'

Always with the nickname. Something he used to rile me up. It was what Maxwell had called the boys, and something they then adopted when talking to me, but after Max died, so did the nickname. Thank fuck.

'The same goes for you, arsehole,' I said, jostling him once more. 'I see you, Grayson Smith, whether you want me to or not, and I know you're just covering up your many issues with alcohol and stupid girls who think they mean something to you.'

'The girls know the drill.'

'Do they? Because that one sucking your dick just now was

telling her friends earlier about how she was going to be the one to hook you.'

'Hook me? Like a duck in one of those carnival games?'

'This isn't a joke!' I stomped my foot, my temper rising, hating that he wasn't taking me seriously. Hating that he rarely took life seriously. 'She had a game plan, and you played right into it.'

'I'm not gonna ask her to be my girlfriend because she can swallow my dick, Ree.'

'*I* know that, arsehole. But those girls are hopeful.'

'Okay, okay. I hear you loud and clear. I'll be a good boy from now on.'

'I'll believe that when I see it,' I replied and opened my car door, got into the driver's seat, and waited for Gray to join me.

Within seconds, he got into the passenger seat and faced me.

'Thanks, Ree,' he said, his bright blue eyes sincere. 'I appreciate you.'

'I know,' I said, not returning the words because I was still a little mad at him. 'Let's blow this joint.'

'Let's.'

Football bored me.

It had never appealed to me and here I was, stuck at the school's football game all because Dad made it clear Rock and I were to attend every school function we could. Sometimes only one of us was necessary, and for the football game, I'd drawn the short straw as Rock and Savannah had plans or some such shit.

Tyler had offered to come along as moral support, but I let him off. None of us cared much about football, so it seemed a little selfish of me to put everybody through the torture of watching dudes run around and kick a ball for ninety minutes.

About ten minutes before the end of the game, I saw my opportunity to sneak off. I'd greeted everyone, done the whole daughter of the school owner thing, and was ready to get the fuck out of there.

On my way out of the stands, I passed Beth Jacobs coming towards me holding two drinks, a deep red flush covering her face. Could be because it was fucking freezing, *but* I also knew that Gray was waiting for me, meaning her flush could be because of him. The boy flirted with anyone, after all. I wanted him to be happy, so of course I wasn't going to ruin anything between him and the new girl, but I also didn't want him hurt either. It was my job as his best friend to help him navigate life without crashing and burning. I smiled at her as I passed and she returned it. Least the girl had manners.

I found Gray waiting in the school car park by my car and I went straight over. 'Thanks for meeting me here. God, that game was such a fucking drag.'

'Seems you managed to slip away a little early at least.'

'I had to, Gray. For my own sanity.' I shook my head, thinking back to the small snippets of the game I remembered. 'I'll just never understand the appeal, you know? Would probably help if I fancied someone on the team, but alas, I do not.'

'Probably because you fancy somebody a little closer to home,' he said, raising his eyebrows. I ignored him and continued past him to my car and got in.

No way was I responding to bullshit like that if I didn't have to.

Gray got in the car, looking contrite. 'Look, if you want me to stop the Rock jokes, I will. I just think the two of you are acting like idiots.'

'Thanks,' I said, my tone dry. Grayson had a knack for digging himself into rather large holes he was unable to get out of without assistance. It was a skill of his. One that sometimes could be considered endearing, and other times could be a massive pain in the arse.

'Ree, you know I just want to see you happy.'

'Right,' I agreed, nodding. 'And I want to see *you* happy, so let's get a move on with this talk you wanted so desperately to have.'

'Okay!' he said, his enthusiasm contagious—almost. 'As we both know, I'm turning eighteen next month.'

'Right…'

'And I'd really like to throw a big massive fuck off party for it.'

'Right…' *Ten guesses as to where this is going.*

'But as we both know, I can't do that at mine. For starters, Dad would never allow it. Plus, the wanker would probably get so wasted he'd embarrass me in front of everyone.'

'Pretty sure you can embarrass yourself enough without any help, but go on.'

He rolled his eyes, but his smile told me he knew I wasn't serious. He jutted out his bottom lip in a pout and started batting his eyelashes before he whined, 'Reeeeee.'

'Yes, Grayson.'

'Can I pretty, pretty please with a thousand cherries on top have my super cool, super hip and happening eighteenth birthday party at your mega mansion?'

'Super hip and happening?' I sputtered. 'You really went with the phrase super hip and happening?'

'Well, it sounded better in my head.'

'I'm sure it did.' I laughed again. 'Do you promise not to get so overly wasted you forget the whole thing?'

'I do.'

'And do you promise not to leave the main house and do something silly like head to the pool house and drown? Or worse, hook up with an unknown girl?'

He had to think about that one a little longer. 'I do.'

'Then fine. You can have your party at my place.' I shook my head, already regretting the decision. 'Dad and Gigi are away that weekend anyway, so that helps. Plus, I'll just add all the food and drink and whatnot onto the weekly housekeeping list.'

'You're a star, Ree! Have I ever told you that?'

'You've mentioned it, yeah.'

'Well, I mean it. I appreciate you.'

Unlike at the field, this time I said it back. 'I appreciate you, too.'

'You coming to the field with me after school?' Gray and I were walking down the school corridor together, arms looped together, and I hoped he was going to say yes. If he didn't go, then I doubted I would either. I was getting bored of having to pretend in social situations that I liked Savannah and her friends. Not that I'd ever actually mastered doing that. Pretty sure I wasn't fooling anybody, least of all myself.

'Nope,' he replied, sounding a lot happier about it than I expected. It was rare for Gray to miss field time, especially when his alternative was going home to his piece of shit dad. 'Got a study session with Jacobs.'

'Since when?' He hadn't mentioned anything to me about study sessions with the new girl. I knew he was failing Science drastically and that he needed help, but it was one subject I couldn't understand for the life of me, so I was no help to him.

'Since I sorted it with her Saturday night.'

'You were with us Saturday night…'

'It's called texting. A form of communication where you don't have to be in the same place as the person you're conversing with.'

'Conversing? You're such a knobhead, Gray,' I said, a small chuckle leaving me before I could rein it in. 'You don't seem anywhere near as miserable as I thought you'd be to have a forced study buddy. What gives?'

'Not like my partner's hideous, is it?'

'She's not hideous,' I agreed, my mind conjuring up the image of Beth Jacobs. She was cute, with long black hair and green eyes that even I could admit were lush. 'But we know nothing about her. Not really.'

'So? Doesn't mean shit about whether she's a good science teacher or not. I *need* to pass, Ree. I can't stay at this shithole for another year and I definitely can't stay with my old man any longer than necessary.'

'I know,' I said, feeling a twinge of guilt for the shit lot Gray was handed in life. It always made me remember my privilege and it made me sick inside that nobody picked the circumstances of their birth. It was just the lot you were drawn. 'Sorry for acting funny. I've just never seen you interested in a girl for more than a quick blowjob behind the trucks at the field.'

'Who said I'm interested?'

'Come off it, Gray. I *know* you, remember? We've been friends since before your mum…' I trailed off, not finishing my sentence. We both knew the blank part. Gray's mum had left years ago and left him alone with an abusive, drunken bastard. I continued, wanting to get back to familiar ground. 'Anyway, I know I haven't seen you smile like this in a while.'

'What about the way you smile when Rock's around, huh?' he teased, taking my hand in his to walk me into the cafeteria, ready to join the long lunch line. 'We just gonna pretend like that doesn't happen?'

'Shut up. There's nothing going on between me and Rock, and you know it. We both know that even if I *did* wanna go there, I couldn't. He's my stepbrother. My dad would lose his shit.'

'Whatever. Let's go get some grub before I literally starve to death.'

'The day you starve to death is the day there's no food left on the planet. You always have at least three snacks in your bag.'

'Who doesn't?' He shrugged. 'Snacks make the world go round.'

'If you say so.'

Twenty

Arianna

age 18, february

It was yet another Friday night, and *yet again*, I found myself over at the field with the guys.

Was I bored with it? Damn straight. But no matter what happened, I still found myself there every week without fail. It was expected of me.

'Just admit it,' I said, standing beside Grayson over by the bonfire. 'You like her.'

The two of us were alone, and off to the side, taking small sips of our drinks, surveying the area. The whole night Gray had kept his eyes locked on the new girl, Beth, and I could see the hunger in his baby blues.

Even if he didn't want to admit shit to me yet.

The girl in question was standing with her best friend Layla, Layla's boyfriend Dean, and their mutual friend Amber, on the other side of the field.

'I don't need to admit it,' Gray said, taking a swig of his beer. 'I already know it.'

I hadn't expected him to come out and say it without any more pre-empting. 'Oh. Saves me a job, I guess.'

'What job's that? The one where you kick me until I'm half-beaten in the grass and admit my feelings for Jacobs?'

'Something like that.' I smiled at the image he'd put in my mind. *Now that sounds kinda fun.*

'Maybe I should do the same for you,' he said and I froze, my cup half-pressed to my lips.

'I don't know what you're talking about.'

'You don't?' His elbow jutted into my ribs and I winced at the contact. *Fucker.* 'We both know you have feelings for Rock, yet won't act on them.'

'He has a girlfriend,' I said through gritted teeth. A girlfriend I'd completely disregarded when I fucked him at the festival, but ya know, swings and roundabouts and all that, right?

'He's only with Savannah because he can't be with you,' Gray pointed out, and even though I half knew the boy was speaking the truth, I didn't want to give him the satisfaction by admitting it.

'I'm sure Savannah would be thrilled if she heard you say that.' My head swung in the direction of Rock and Savannah. The two of them were standing close together, his arm wrapped tight around her waist, as they listened to something Spencer was getting animated about. 'He's my stepbrother. Can you imagine our parents if we started dating? They'd freak and then probably take our money away while they were at it.'

'Probably,' he agreed. 'But when you weigh it up, what matters to you more, money or happiness?'

'Don't get all head shrink on me. We're not talking about *me*.'

'I don't need you to tell me how I feel,' he said, moving back to the thought of Beth. 'I've accepted that I like Jacobs and I wanna see what can happen.'

'Wow,' I said, a little shocked. 'You *do* like her.'

He rolled his eyes at me. 'I literally just told you that.'

'No, but I mean, you *really* like her if you're willing to see where it goes. You kissed her in front of everyone.' The moment he'd done it, the crowd had hushed. It was like people were waiting for the world to implode or something else super dramatic.

'I've done more than kiss a girl in front of a crowd before.'

'And every day I wish I could scrub my eyes from the sights they've seen.'

We both broke out into laughter, and I watched as Gray made a salute with his beer bottle in Beth's direction, then watched transfixed as Beth raised her cup back before taking a sip.

'Jesus, Gray, you're smitten,' I said, a small giggle leaving me. I realised I was happy for him, even if I was a little sour that I couldn't have the same as him with the person my heart had given itself too—without permission, I'd like to add.

'Oh, fuck off.'

'What I meant is you kissed her in front of everyone at the start of the evening. You claimed her in front of all the guys who may have tried hitting on her.' He opened his mouth to interrupt me, but I held up my finger. No way was he stopping me in my flow. '*Plus*, you made it clear to any girl here that you're taken.'

'Did I?'

'You just put a target over that girl's head,' I said, not liking the way he was acting so innocent—like he didn't know what he was doing.

'Bit dramatic even for you, Ree.'

'Every girl here is gonna wanna know what she did to get your attention. And every girl here is gonna give her hell for it. She's still the new girl.'

'They won't. Otherwise, we'll make it clear she's off-limits. Last time I checked, we still had a reputation.'

One we were hanging on to by a thread, I thought.

But all I said was, 'One we didn't do shit to earn.'

'Doesn't matter whether we *earned* it or if Maxwell handed it to us on a silver platter,' Gray stressed. 'People listen to us.'

'Guess I should probably make nice with her.' Not that I was mean to her or anything, because I wasn't. I just hadn't got to know her super well yet, but if Gray was into her, then I'd do my best.

'If you could.'

'I find girls hard to get along with,' I admitted, twisting my hands together.

'I know, but this one's different. It isn't like I'm asking you to befriend the girl who sucked my dick that night you interrupted.'

'Grayson! Do you have to put pictures like that into my head every day? I've seen your dick way too many times for a best friend.' *Way too many times.*

'Sorry about it,' he said with a laugh, not sounding apologetic one bit. 'You know you love me.'

'Be easier if I didn't.'

'Hush up, you,' he said, twirling a strand of my hair around his index finger before his face became thoughtful. 'You gonna stay tonight?'

'And listen to Rock and Savannah in a tent together? No fucking thank you. I'd rather listen to classical music and watch ballet.' Not that I'd heard them any other week since the festival, but I wasn't going to take any chances.

I used to do ballet when I was younger—something I was super into—but after I was pushed over during a recital, I didn't want to do it anymore. It was one of my greatest embarrassments.

'Wow. Serious stuff.'

'When you reckon you'll get Beth all to yourself?' I asked, surveying the area and noticing that a lot of kids were starting to float off and do their own thing. It wouldn't be long until I could do the same and it wouldn't look too suspicious.

'Few hours' time, I'd say. Her friends won't leave this early and I'm not gonna be the kind of dickhead who takes her away from them if she's having fun.'

If I thought I'd been shocked before, then he was pushing me over the edge. 'I'm sorry, but who are you and what have you done with Grayson Smith?'

'I'm serious, Ree. I don't wanna fuck this up before we've

even got started. She'll come to me when she's ready, and I've got the whole weekend with her pretty much, so I'm good.'

'I'm glad.' His birthday party was the next night and I guess he planned to spend that night with her, too. 'I'm happy to see you smile, Gray.'

And I meant it.

'Now we just need to work on your smile,' he told me, his eyes narrowing on my face, but I just gritted my teeth and shook my head.

'We may both be waiting a long time.'

'How's it going, princess?' Tyler's face came into view, the dying flames from the bonfire flickering on his features, and I smiled at him, happy he'd come to my side.

Gray had headed off to be with Beth and I was yet to leave the field, as if something unknown to me was making me stay.

'It's going,' I said, looking up into his wide eyes. 'How's the night treating you?'

'It's treating,' he said with a laugh. 'Saw you talking to Gray earlier. Anything exciting?'

'Not much. Just that he likes the new girl.'

'Well, I think the whole field understood that when he kissed her in front of everyone.'

'That's what *I* told him!' I said, nodding. 'Told him he'd put a target on the poor girl's head.'

'You're not wrong,' he agreed. 'Poor girl won't know what hit her.'

We both fell silent. The only sound was the dying embers from the fire, but it wasn't uncomfortable or awkward. If anything, it felt natural. Right.

And that thought scared me.

'You spoke to Rock recently?' Ty asked and my gaze narrowed at the mere mention of his name.

'You know I haven't,' I snapped, pissed that he was making me mad when I'd had a pretty Rock and Savannah free evening thus far. 'Not since he invited Sucky Savannah to my birthday.'

'Actually, princess, that was me.'

'Fine then.' I huffed. 'Not since he invited Suck Savannah's *friends* to my birthday.'

'Yeah,'—he chuckled, running his hand through his hair—'I definitely didn't invite those girls.'

'I think he thinks we're dating,' I said out of nowhere.

The thought had been running through my mind for some time, most likely ever since our disastrous four-way trip to mini golf, and even though Rock had never outright told me he thought something was going on with me and Tyler, I got the impression that he believed *something* more was happening.

'Oh, I'm one hundred percent sure he thinks we're dating, yeah,' Tyler said, his large smile infectious. 'Isn't that what we wanted?'

I thought about his question.

Was that what I wanted?

I shrugged. 'I'm not sure, honestly.'

'After I found you at the festival, I thought we were on the same page.' Ty reached out and placed his finger under my chin, tilting my face up so we were making eye contact. 'Even if the lines get blurred every now and then.'

I chuckled. The boy wasn't wrong about lines getting blurred between us sometimes, but whenever the thoughts slipped in, I made sure they danced straight back out again. I didn't need to want two people I couldn't have.

It was Tyler who'd stumbled across me after Rock left me— rejected me—by the fairground and even though we hadn't spoken about it much after, I knew if I did want to talk about it, Tyler would be all ears.

'Well, I'm happy that the lines are blurred with you and nobody else.'

'That has to be one of the nicest things you've ever said to me, princess.'

'Oh, shut your face.' The heel of my hand connected with his shoulder and we both laughed. I wished it *was* Tyler I had a crush on, because maybe then things would be a whole heck of a lot easier. 'You know what I mean.'

Which would be impressive, really, seeing as I had absolutely no clue when I meant, but it sounded like the right thing to say.

'You looking forward to tomorrow?'

'Fuck no,' I said. 'But I know Gray will love it, and honestly, that's what matters. The boy doesn't exactly win the life of the year awards, does he?'

'Harsh.'

'But true,' I stressed. 'It's the least I could do for him.'

'You're a doll, princess. Anyone ever told you that?'

I just rolled my eyes, happy to be by Tyler's side, all while pretending that I couldn't see Rock and Savannah's faces locked together in a passionate kiss on the other side of the field from us.

Maybe if I pretended they didn't exist enough, they'd disappear.

Wishful thinking.

Twenty-One

Arianna

age 18, february

FOR MAYBE THE HUNDREDTH TIME, I wondered why the fuck I'd told Grayson he could throw his eighteenth birthday party at my house.

'Sorry, love!' the guy who'd pushed my back so I bumped into the counter hollered, his drink spilling out of his plastic cup onto the floor, and I winced.

Ace and I were hiding out in the kitchen, as he mixed one of his world-famous cocktails for me. Meaning that it was famous in *his* world: Beurre.

On my way to the kitchen, I'd walked past Spencer and Tyler standing with Remi over by the fireplace, an argument having just broken out between them, and I glided past as fast as I could. Nobody needed to get caught up in their crap. I already had enough crap on my plate as it was.

Rock was dancing in the middle of the room with Savannah hanging off him, and I'd walked even faster past them, basically breaking out into a run.

Things were still tense between us.

After the conversation we had after slipping up and having sex at Beurrefest, I knew he liked Savannah. Knew that he wasn't faking it half as much as I'd thought he was, but that didn't mean it didn't still hurt.

'Here you are!' Ace said, handing me the drink he'd been working on for the last ten minutes.

Better be fucking worth it.

A glass smashed in the living room, and we both looked at each other, a question in our eyes: *Are we going to go check that out?*

Then we laughed and shook our heads. Whatever it was wasn't worth our time. I'd already spent the majority of the night acting uptight and it had got me nowhere.

'Cheers.' I grabbed the glass and clinked it with his. 'And thanks for keeping me company. I'm surprised you're not with the guys.'

'Well, Spencer got it into his head that he needed to talk to Remi, and I wasn't joining him for that.' Ace shook his head. 'We all miss Max, you know? But it's not like Remi was his girlfriend when he died.'

I gave a grunt of agreement, not wanting to touch that sentence with my opinion. Because, unlike the others, I couldn't say truthfully that I missed Max. If anything, I was happy he was no longer around to torment me for being the only girl in our group.

Remi stormed into the room, bumping into Ace, a scowl on her face.

'Watch where you're going,' Ace growled. Remi's response was to laugh, a cackle really, high-pitched and derisive. The hatred she felt towards us both was thick in the air, and I rolled my eyes, wondering when she'd become such a bitch. Remi had always been popular, but in the last couple of years it had only got worse, and it had definitely gone to her very fake, very bleached, blonde head.

'Not like I walked into you on purpose,' she spat, checking behind her to see if anybody had followed her. 'I would apologise, but you're not worth it.'

With a flick of her hair, she went outside, leaving Ace standing there with his jaw agape.

'Somebody needs to knock that girl down a peg.'

'Get in line,' Tyler murmured, appearing in the kitchen with a bottle of beer gripped in his hand. 'I've got plans.'

'Whatever, dude.' Ace took a sip of his cocktail, his irritation at Remi already forgotten. 'Now *this* is a cocktail!'

Having been dismissed, Tyler followed Remi outside, and a small part of me that loved drama wanted to follow and find out what *that* was all about, but then somebody else entered the kitchen and distracted me.

The newcomer wasn't somebody I'd seen before.

He definitely didn't attend Hollowdale High. I'd have remembered if he did.

His hair was a light golden brown, and his eyes were dark and piercing, cutting through me like he could see into my soul.

He was gorgeous.

And *new*.

And quite obviously filthy, stinking rich.

His clothes screamed wealth, as did the expensive cologne he'd put on. Having grown up in wealthier circles due to my dad's business pursuits, I wasn't intimidated by him. If anything, I sort of pitied him.

'Do you mind making me one of those?' he asked me, pointing at the glass in my hand.

'You think because I'm a girl, I made this?' I asked with bite. Of course he had to be one of those gorgeous guys who was a major misogynist. It was hard to find somebody so *handsome* who wasn't a prick, too.

'Shit, you're right,' he said with a small laugh. 'I was a right prick then, wasn't I?'

At least he knows it.

'You bet.'

'Can I be candid?' he asked, and I nodded. What on earth

was this rich dude about to say to me? 'I just wanted an excuse to talk to you.'

'So, you went with the "she's the girl, she must've made the drink" angle?' I quirked an eyebrow at him, pointing out just how stupid that logic sounded when you voiced it plainly.

'Right.' He chuckled. 'When you say it out loud, it sounds a lot worse than it sounded in my head.'

'I'm sure it does.' Ace laughed, watching between the two of us as if we'd become his favourite tennis match. 'I'll make you one'—then he paused, looking the random guy up and down —'if you actually want the drink, that is?'

The guy nodded at Ace. 'Please.'

Ace turned away from the two of us and went back to his spot at the counter, in his element, and no doubt wanting to prove that his 'world-famous' cocktail held up with strangers as well as those who loved him and just made him happy by praising him.

'So…' I crossed my arms over my chest, ready to start probing him with intrusive questions if need be. 'Who are you?'

'Wouldn't you like to know?'

'Yes,' I said, blunt as fuck. 'That's why I asked.'

He laughed, as if I wasn't being serious. 'I think it's more exciting if I stay a mystery. You seem like the kind of girl who doesn't like mysteries.'

'And once again you're making an assumption about me, yet you know nothing about me.'

'I know this is your house,' he said, his top lip curling up at the corner, his eyes warm with humour. 'I know your name is Arianna.'

'Ah, but you don't know *me*. Anybody could've told you those things.'

'I know enough to know I want to know more.'

'Smooth.'

'I try.' He chuckled again and as much as I thought he was a bit smarmy, I was also disarmed by his banter. There was something about a guy who could find humour even in the bleakest of times. 'But seriously. I saw you across the room and wanted to know you.'

'Well, here I am,' I said, swooping my arm out. 'Hope my winning banter and charm is everything you hoped it'd be.'

His smile was wide, and it sent flutters through my stomach, it was that fucking beautiful. His teeth were bright, straight, and that told me he came from money more than anything else.

Ace handed Handsome his drink and he took a small sip. Once he knew it wasn't poison or about to kill him, he drank more.

'Thanks, mate.' He gave Ace a nod and turned back to me. 'Want to head outside? Bet it's quieter out there.'

Remi and Tyler had gone out back not too long ago, but it was my fucking garden, so I wasn't going to let their trashy antics stop me from leaving the kitchen with a stranger. Not that I thought Tyler was trashy. He was one of my closest friends and clearly I needed to talk to him about whatever was going on with him.

'I doubt it's much quieter, but sure. I know all the hiding spots, after all.'

His arm reached out and I took his hand in mine, the spirits in the cocktail surging through my body and warming me. I wasn't acting like myself. I didn't just go off with random guys to hidden spots. Fuck, I didn't even do that with non-random guys I'd known for years.

Not that I didn't hook up with guys.

Okay, that may be me stretching the truth a tiny bit. Since I hooked up with Tyler a couple of times at the field, I hadn't really hooked up with anyone. Nobody appealed to me—well, nobody that wasn't my stepbrother at least.

But the stranger holding my hand and leading me out the door to the garden was a good place to start.

TWENTY-TWO
ROCK

age 18, february

I FINALLY GOT AWAY from dealing with Spencer's drunk arse, having put him in one of the empty bedrooms upstairs, and made my way into the kitchen.

I should really be looking for Savannah, but my mind had another girl on its mind—one who didn't have blonde hair. And she definitely didn't call herself my girlfriend, either.

'Yo,' Ace called as I entered. 'Where's your girl?'

'I thought you were in here with her,' I replied, then blanched at the words I'd let stumble from my lips. *Shit.* I coughed. 'I mean, I thought I saw Savannah come in here. You seen her?'

'No…' His eyes narrowed on my face, and I hoped the flush wasn't that obvious on my cheeks. 'I haven't seen Sav, but Ari's outside with a guy if you were looking for her, too.'

The bastard saw right through me.

Fuck, these days everybody did. They all just remained silent about it. Think Gray's words were, *one day they'll get their heads out of their arses and see what we see.*

'A guy?'

'Yeah. Never seen him before. He just swanned over to her and struck up a convo. Knew her name and everything.'

'What's his name?'

Ace rubbed his jaw, scratching the slight bit of stubble he kept as he believed it made him look older, and my stomach sank.

'Well, now that you mention it, mate, he didn't say his name at all.'

The more Ace said, the more dread filled me. Ari didn't hook up with guys. She didn't go off with random ones who didn't even tell her their name. She wasn't acting like herself, and I wasn't in a position to go up to her and confront her about it.

Fuck, I should be trying to find my *girlfriend*, not my stepsister.

I picked up a glass from the counter in front of Ace and drank the contents, not giving a fuck about what was in it, needing the haze of alcohol to wipe away the thoughts swirling through my brain.

'Hey, babe,' a voice slurred as arms came around my waist. Guess I knew where my girlfriend was. 'I've been looking for you.'

'I had to handle Spencer,' I replied, leaning back into her. 'The boy was pissed at Remi. You know, the usual.'

'No, actually, I don't know,' she said, with a brittle laugh that gave away her true feelings. 'You forget that I don't know the ins and outs of you "Rebels".'

Her scorn knocked me back and I turned to face her, a question in my eyes. Savannah and I had been together for long enough now that I thought she'd got used to my group of friends—but clearly not. She was more than happy to drink with them and play games with them at Beurrefest, after all.

'I didn't mean it like that,' she said, her face falling slightly in an apology of sorts, and my stomach twisted with something that felt a little like pity but also could've been indigestion. She went up on her tiptoes and whispered in my ear, 'Want to get out of here?'

'Right now?'

She nodded, kissing my neck.

'I've barely even seen the birthday boy.'

Like I gave a fuck about seeing a wasted Grayson. I'd seen enough of that shit show for a lifetime.

Sav took her lips off my skin and said, 'Oh, I just saw him. He's about to head upstairs with that girl he's been drooling over.'

'Beth?'

'The new girl?' she asked, twirling her hair around her finger, and I nodded. 'Yeah, her.'

'If he's taking her upstairs, I really should tell Ari about it.'

'Why? Is she his keeper?'

'No, but—'

'So, leave them alone,' Sav said, exasperated at my friends, or maybe at me? Who knew with her. One second, she was happy, the next bitter and ticked off about something or other. 'Gray's an adult now. Any decision he makes is for him to deal with. Not you.'

'I suppose.'

'You know I'm right, Boo.' She reached up and kissed my lips in a gentle caress. 'How about we get out of here?'

'I live here,' I said, wondering if she'd really had that much to drink and I just hadn't noticed. 'And I should stay in case shit gets worse. If Gray and Ari have abandoned ship, then I should stick around and make sure nobody ruins my mum's leather sofas or whatnot.'

A sound of derision came from the back of Savannah's throat and I bristled. Whether she liked it or not, the party was happening in *my* house and I couldn't leave—even if I wanted to.

But the main reason I didn't want to leave with Sav?

I wanted to go find Ari to see where she and the stranger had disappeared to. A stranger who hadn't even given her his name. What the fuck was she even thinking?

And the thing that killed me the most?

The fact I had no control over what she did, who she spoke

to, or any of it. *Not* that I'd control her if she was mine, but you get me.

'We could go up to your bedroom,' she said, placing small kisses down my neck, 'and then we'd still be here.'

'But we wouldn't be watching, would we?' I murmured, toying with the idea she'd planted in my mind.

Fuck. I'm an awful human.

Ever since I'd had sex with Ari at the festival, I hadn't fucked Savannah due to some kind of moral code I was running on, but with Ari off God knows where with a guy, my patience and self-control were wearing thin. And fuck did that make me a prick.

'What's to watch? Kids grinding on each other while their friends puke out front? Come on, babe. Ari and Gray decided to throw this party, so it's on them to clear up any messes, isn't it?'

With each sentence, she was twisting my arm—poisoning me to listen to her and abandon my post. Because she was right, wasn't she?

I hadn't agreed to the party, not really, but it wasn't like I was going to say no to one of my best mates and the girl I'd had a crush on forever.

'I guess you're right...' I trailed off and she pounced on my indecision.

'I'm always right.' Her smile made me feel warm inside, like she was smiling and it was sinking into my veins, giving me a high the alcohol hadn't.

'Come on,' I said, trailing my hand down her ribcage to her waist before grabbing her hand in mine, ready to lead her to my bedroom. 'Let's get outta dodge.'

'Finally!'

Twenty-Three
Arianna

age 18, february

'So…' I asked as we walked out into the garden and down the path that led to the pool house. 'You're not from around here?'

'I am, actually,' he said with a small chuckle, endearing himself to me even more. 'I live in the Hills too.'

'Huh,' I said, stumped. The way Hawthorn Hills was laid out, the majority of people knew one another—or at least *of* one another. *Handsome*, the name I'd given him in my head as he hadn't told me his name yet, wasn't somebody I'd seen around and he definitely didn't go to school with me, which made him a complete mystery. 'Whereabouts?'

'A couple of streets over,' he replied, a step behind, letting me take the lead. 'My family and I are new-ish to the area.'

'That explains it then.'

'Explains what?'

'Why I've never seen you around.'

'And you'd have recognised me, would you?'

'Are you fishing for a compliment?'

'Maybe…' He chuckled, squeezing my hand. 'I'll take whatever you give me.'

'Okay, handsome. Whatever you say.'

'Handsome?'

'Well, you've not told me your name and I need to call you *something*.'

'Now that I know you're calling me handsome, I'm not going to tell you my actual name.'

'Suit yourself.' I shrugged, the epitome of nonchalance to disguise how badly I wanted to know who the fuck he was.

But it would ruin the mystery, and it wasn't like I planned to see him again once he left.

When we turned the corner by the greenhouse, I saw Remi Riley pressed up against the greenhouse wall, some guy I couldn't see the face of kissing her neck.

Not getting involved in that shit.

I turned us back around, hotfooting it in the opposite direction.

'Where are you taking me?' His voice was like velvet. Smooth and sending shivers down my spine—but in a *very* good way.

'I wasn't taking you anywhere in particular.'

'You seem like a woman on a mission.'

'And what's that even supposed to mean?' I laughed, wondering why the phrase irked me so much. Why was a determined female always such a threat or something to comment upon?

Before he could answer me, the first splash of rain hit out of nowhere, landing on my cheek. You know that kind of rain that was actually rain and not super fine or whatever? It was like that. Proper large dollops of water that would soak you through within minutes.

'Oh shit!' I shouted, covering my face with my hands. 'Follow me.'

I turned the lights on in the pool house and shuffled inside, seeking shelter from the downpour that had come out of nowhere.

Everything inside was clean and untouched, waiting for somebody to come inside and fill it with warmth.

It was the one place Gigi hadn't got her hands on. Meaning it didn't resemble the tunnel of love or some other hideous carnival attraction like the spare room in my house did.

'Welcome,' I said, sweeping my hand out. 'Step inside.'

'Is this where you kill me?'

'Maybe. Guess you'll have to stick around and find out.'

'Let me get this straight,' he said, stepping inside the house. 'Either I stay outside and get completely drenched, or I come inside and get murdered by a striking woman?'

'Are you trying to flatter me so I don't kill you?'

'Is it working?'

'I'll let you know in half an hour,' I joked. Even if Rock's mum never entered the house, our housekeeper definitely did, so the fridge was stocked with drinks and there was some food in a couple of the cupboards. 'Want a drink?'

Handsome was taking in the house, wandering around close behind me, and I couldn't help but smile at the turn of events. I hadn't wanted to spend the night watching Rock and Savannah together, but I also hadn't wanted to babysit Gray either.

I hoped he wasn't doing anything too stupid. Maybe I should head back...

But then arms came around my waist and I decided Gray had turned eighteen, meaning he was an adult, and he could cope for one night without me there cleaning up his messes. Right?

'What are you thinking so deeply about?' He turned me around so I was facing him, and I shuffled an inch back so I wouldn't be quite so pressed up against his body. A body I hadn't had much time to peruse, but now found myself doing so. He was slim, athletic, and even though he didn't have large arm muscles like Rock, he still had defined abs lurking underneath his tight T-shirt.

I shook myself before my thoughts took a turn for the dirty. 'Just my friend Gray. Wondering if I should head back to the main house and make sure he hasn't drowned in a pool of his own vomit or something.'

'Is that a likely occurrence?'

'With Grayson, you never know.'

'He's the guy whose party it is?'

I nodded.

'And the two of you are… close?'

'The closest,' I affirmed. 'We've been friends forever, and I just can't shake the fucker.'

'Would you want to?'

'Nope,' I said with a laugh, trying to imagine a Grayson-less life and not being able to. 'He makes my life interesting, ya know? Without him, I'd be sitting at home, alone, reading or watching TV to pass the time. Do you have a friend like that?'

It was a blatant fish for more information on the stranger I'd let into my home, but he didn't bite.

'I don't really have many friends,' he said, his tone low, and a twinge of sadness flickered in his pupils. 'Not in the area, at least.'

'When did you move to Hawthorn Hills?'

'Last month. Before then, I lived a couple of towns over, but Dad decided it was time to come here. Something to do with business contacts living here or something.' He shrugged, the gesture of a child who had no idea about their parents' business shit but having to go along with it anyway. There were plenty of times where I'd found myself at an event or dinner because Dad told me he needed me there. Usually, it was because the guy he was trying to charm—read swindle—had a kid around my age he thought I could impress.

'My dad's the same,' I confided. 'Always focused on business and not much else.'

'What business is your dad in? Must be something pretty big to live in a place like this.' He gestured around us. 'Even on this side of the divide, there aren't many houses bigger than this.'

The 'divide', as it was known, ran right through the centre of Beurre, and therefore right down the centre of Hollowdale High. It was aptly named the divide as it signified the split between the wealthier side of town and the side that wasn't. Rock used to live on the other side of the divide before his mum married my dad, and Gray still lived there. Our school had pupils from both sides, and that was one of the main reasons Rock and I had never gone to Hawthorn Academy, the private school up on the hill. Dad couldn't exactly advertise Hollowdale as a diverse place of learning if he chose to send his own children elsewhere.

'You may not have been here long, and you may not have many friends, but you clearly know something if you're referring to it as the divide.'

'I heard a kid talking about it when I arrived. Something about how parties on this side of the divide were always better.'

'Makes sense. A lot of kids say that, but I don't agree with them.'

'Why not?'

'Because, for starters, parties on this side are all about people wanting to show off how rich they are. How much space they have. That kind of shit. Whereas house parties and field parties where wealth isn't the main focus are always more genuine. Real friends having real fun. None of that look at me crap.'

'But *you* threw this party.'

'Only because my best friend asked me to. Plus, he knew if I threw the party, I'd be able to swing free booze, and Grayson will show up *literally anywhere* if it includes free alcohol.'

'As would the rest of the town, it would seem.' We laughed, and I took a bottle of water out of the fridge, uncapped it, and took a sip, hoping it would cool down the warmth in my blood. Just being in a space with a boy I didn't know, alone, was starting to bring my anxiety levels up.

The rain had stopped outside, and I knew I should mention leaving to head back to the main house, but I stopped myself.

For one night, I could be somebody else. I could hang out with a guy I didn't know and enjoy his company, then never speak to him again.

Other girls my age did it, like Remi, so maybe I needed to take a leaf out of their books and be carefree for once. Stop worrying so much about what people thought of me, or what would happen if it got back to my dad.

If my dad gave a shit about me, he'd be here, but he wasn't—he never was.

The alcohol had made me bold, so it only made sense when I uttered the sentence, 'Want to come upstairs with me?'

THE SUN WAS SHINING through the large floor-to-ceiling glass panes, and I couldn't keep my eyes closed any longer.

I could sense from the moment I'd awoken that the space on the bed next to me was empty, and for a brief second, my heart sank—but only for a second. Handsome had been exactly that, handsome as fuck, but the whole evening had played out like a dream. A fantasy of sorts.

One where I was the chosen girl and somebody went out of their way to make me feel special, like I mattered the most, and as much as I enjoyed it for the few hours it existed, I wasn't sure I'd want that kind of attention in the morning, too.

With him gone, I didn't have to play out the awkward morning after where we both pretended we wanted to see each other again, and there would be none of those uncomfortable questions I didn't know how to answer.

Once we went upstairs into the bedroom, things had gotten pretty heated a lot faster than I'd intended. The moment we were through the door, it was as if a weight was lifted from us both and we were able to be our most primal selves.

It was liberating.

And completely out of character for me.

My hand reached across to the bedside table where I'd thrown my phone and hadn't looked at it since. *Shit.* I had over twenty missed calls and multiple unread texts—mainly from Rock. There were also a couple sprinkled in from Ace and Tyler, too. The messages were all along a similar vein but delivered in a completely different way.

> Ace - Where you got to? Ya boy's freaking.

> Ty - Princess, let me know where you are, okay? Rumour has it you went off with a stranger… I'm crushed

> Rock - Ari. Ace told me he saw you go off with a guy who didn't even let you know his name. Where the fuck are you?

> Rock - I'm in my room, waiting to hear you return safe. Message me if you need anything, okay? No matter what time it is.

> Rock - Don't freeze me out, ice queen. Text me.

> Rock - Just let me know you're safe.

Ace hadn't specified what boy was freaking, but from the look of the texts, it wasn't Tyler he was referring to. Ty's text made me laugh, knowing he wasn't crushed in the slightest. Not really.

Rock's texts sent a stone hurtling to the bottom of my stomach, landing at the bottom with a painful thud. The last time I spotted him before meeting Handsome, he was breaking up the fight in the living room, but before that, Savannah was attached to him like a bad smell and nobody else could get close enough.

Even though he was the one with the girlfriend, I still felt guilty as shit about my actions.

Suppose it was time to head back to the main house and face the music... even if I didn't want to *at all*.

TWENTY-FOUR
ROCK

age 18, february

'Where were you?'

The words flew from my mouth in accusation, and even though I knew I should take it back and ask it a little nicer, I didn't.

Ari's eyes met mine across the kitchen counter, narrowed and slightly aggravated.

'What?'

It always amazed me how she could cut me with one word and one word only.

The delivery giving all of her thoughts and opinions away in a moment.

'Where were you last night?'

'Here.' She crossed her arms in front of her chest, pushing her tits up, and like the total tool I am, I couldn't resist looking. She noticed my eyeline and shifted, covering herself. 'Last time I checked, we threw a party last night, remember?'

'I didn't mean that and you know it.' Or at least I hoped she knew it because I wasn't sure I'd be able to explain what I meant in a way that made sense and didn't make me sound like a massive wanker.

'Well, enlighten me, *Drew*. What exactly do you mean?'

I'd ruffled her if she was resorting to using my name. Ari only ever brought out the big guns (a.k.a. my true name) when she was feeling feisty and ready for a fight.

'I couldn't find you last night,' I mumbled, feeling more of a jerk the more I spoke. 'Ace told me you were out in the garden with some guy, but then I didn't see you afterwards at all.'

Not that I'd looked after Savannah convinced me to go upstairs with her… but Ari didn't know that. And I'd expected to hear her bedroom door close, seeing as it was the room next to mine, even staying up later than I wanted to make sure she got back okay, but she never showed.

'We stayed out in the pool house.'

'Oh.' *We.* 'Who is we?'

'You already know,' she said, pointing at me in accusation. 'You told me just now. I was with *some guy*. Right?'

'You're pissed.'

'Rock, I just came into the room and you're throwing shitty, demanding questions at me about where I was last night. Of course I'm pissed at that.' She shrugged, looking resigned. 'If you asked nicely, I would've told you all about it.'

The words were telling me one thing—but the look on her face was telling another. There was no way she had any intention of telling me about the night before.

Fuck.

The two of us barely speak, and especially not completely alone like we were at that moment.

Ever since the events of that summer, Ari had avoided me like I was deadly. And maybe to a degree, I was.

She'd made it clear that what happened at the festival could never happen again, no matter how much we may have both wanted it to.

'So, tell me all about it now,' I said, desperate to get myself back into her good graces. 'Our rents don't get back for another couple of days. We can order in food and eat in the living room on the sofas my mum said we can't eat food on ever. Watch a film or some trashy reality TV. Whatever you want. Just don't ice me out anymore.'

'I don't *ice you out*.'

'You sure about that?'

She nodded.

'Then what would you call it, Miss Ice Queen?'

Her mouth spread into a thin-lipped smile, and I could see the restraint in her features. Oh yeah. Ari wanted to rip my head off.

And honestly, I'd probably let her if it meant she was close enough to touch.

'Are you trying to piss me off on purpose?'

'Maybe.' I smirked. 'Is it working?'

She laughed, loud, and I joined in, a thrill shooting through me at having made her laugh—a real, genuine laugh, not one of the fake ones she doled out to people she didn't give a shit about impressing.

'You're paying for food.'

'Of course.'

'And I get to choose what we have.'

'Sure.'

'Plus, the TV choice is all mine, too.'

'Whatever you say, ice queen.'

'Stop calling me that!'

'Nope.' I shook my head. 'I think I'll keep using it, actually. Your reaction makes it worth risking your wrath.'

'You really do know how to piss me off, don't you, dickhead?'

'Ari,' I said, taking a couple of steps closer to where she was still standing, rooted to the spot, arms crossed. 'I live for it.'

'Well, maybe you should live for something else, like, oh, I don't know, your girlfriend.'

The words hit me the way she'd intended. Like a knife in the gut, slicing downwards, until my insides were out in the open.

Everybody made mistakes in life.

I'd just happened to make more than others.

'Want me to invite her?' I asked, not wanting her to see how much she flayed me. 'Sure, she'd be up for a ménage a trois.'

'Just what I've always wanted,' Ari deadpanned before turning away to walk out of the room without a backwards glance. 'I'll let you know what food I want.'

'Ari!' I called out, wanting her to turn back around—wanting our conversation to go back to an easy-going flow rather than the brittle thing it had become.

'I'll be down in an hour. Don't follow me.' Her voice was already far enough away that I knew she'd reached the large ornate staircase in the entrance hallway. Even all these years later, it still felt surreal to live in such a mansion. To have my every whim and want paid for without my having to do anything for it, except to breathe.

I wished I could place the time when things went so wrong between me and Ari. Was it when we became stepsiblings or sometime after that?

Shit.

It had been the first time we'd spoken just us two for a while and I'd managed to fuck it up in a way only I could, when all I wanted was for us to go back to the way we'd been before hormones got in the way. Before my brain—and not my brain— had decided she was the most beautiful and most sexy girl in existence.

Double shit.

I shouldn't be thinking that way. Especially not with a girl-friend whose text I had ignored about hanging out that night.

Well. I'd always known I was a massive arsehole, so I guess it made sense to live up to that.

AFTER AN HOUR, she came downstairs to the kitchen as if things weren't tense between us both. As if I hadn't done nothing for the past hour while waiting for her to return.

'Want me to order in?' she asked, a peace offering of sorts in a way only Arianna could pull off. 'I'll even let you choose where from.'

'Somebody's feeling guilty.'

Ari winced and fidgeted on the spot, her fingers fiddling with the bottom of her T-shirt.

'Next you'll be telling me I can choose what we watch, too.'

The way her face scrunched told me she'd been about to do just that.

I chuckled at her. After so many years of knowing her, I knew her tells. Knew when she was feeling bad, mad, or happy, and at that moment, she was for sure oozing with guilt. 'If you're offering, I want sushi!'

'Really?' she whined, turning her narrowed eyes to me in accusation. 'That's really, genuinely what you want? Of all the food places that exist, that's what you're going for?'

'Yep,' I replied. 'You know it's one of my favourites, and you don't hate it either!'

'No, I don't hate it,' she grumbled. 'It's just we have to order *so* much of it for it to fill either of us up. Especially you! You eat it all before I've even had the chance to take a bite of everything.'

'Because you're stingy when it comes to ordering!' I accused, pointing a finger at her. 'When you order, double what you think is enough and then maybe add another portion or two of something extra.'

She rolled her eyes and it made me laugh more. Getting under her skin was a joy, but also, I knew she'd take it because she'd scared me the night before when I didn't know where she was.

'I'll order enough for a football team then, shall I?'

'That sounds good to me.' I stepped closer to her, rubbing my hands together, my stomach grumbling at the thought of devouring enough sushi to feed a small army. 'Order the usual items and I'll be in the cinema room picking out a film.'

'No need to look so happy about it.' Her bottom lip jutted out in a pout and I couldn't move my eyes away quick enough. When she noticed my gaze, Ari pulled it back in, her eyes downcast.

'Maybe next time you'll at least let me know where you are.'

'You're not my keeper.'

I took another step towards her, but instead of backing away like she usually did, she stood her ground. It made me want to push her further. To not back down for once.

'I thought you said you were going to pick a film.' Her voice was barely above a whisper, and a sharp thrill ran through me at the tension in the air. We could both sense it—it was so potent there was no denying it. 'Shoo.'

'Make me,' I whispered, close enough now to reach out and trail my fingertips down her cheek to her once more pouting lips.

'Rock.' My name was a plea. 'You're not playing fair.'

'When have I ever played fair?'

Her smile was thin-lipped and taut. 'How am I supposed to react? How am I supposed to act around you? One day, you're cold and the next you're so fucking hot I need to step away for my sanity.'

'You think I'm fucking hot?'

The flush of pink that entered her cheeks made her look softer somehow, younger, and I knew I shouldn't act so strong with her, but I couldn't help it. Sometimes actions were compulsions.

My face was within touching distance of hers and I took full advantage of the situation, pressing my lips on hers, gentle but with enough pressure she could decide whether to reciprocate.

And reciprocate she did.

Pressure met mine, and then all bets were off. Our lips moved in a well-established rhythm, one we had figured out before, and everything about the moment felt right. Predestined. Like it was meant to happen.

But before my tongue could slip inside her mouth, she paused and moved away from my lips to assess my face.

'You know you're hot,' she muttered, ignoring the brief kiss. 'But yes, Rock. I think you're hot.' Her step back was sign enough that she didn't want to repeat it.

'For some reason, ice queen, it feels a lot better coming from your lips than any others.' I tried to sound jovial, but it came out rather flat.

'Guess you want me to take that as a compliment of sorts?' Her fingers were warm on my forearm, and I froze at her touch, not expecting it but wanting it all the same. Whenever she touched me, my body came alive. As if all the nerve endings and synapses and whatever the fuck else that existed inside a human body remembered they were alive. 'But it's a little hard to take anything you say seriously when you haven't even ended shit with Savannah yet.'

'It's hard.'

'Living is hard, Rock!' she shouted, a roar of anger I barely saw from her. 'Being your sister is hard! Having to stay away from you because of our parents is hard! But you know what's not hard? Staying single on the off chance that one day we can become reality!'

I was taken aback by the hatred in her words, by the anger on her face, and the tension in her body. Even her bright red hair in a ponytail seemed to stop swinging for once.

I'm a prick.

How had I never thought about her single status as something she chose because she was waiting for me?

I'd just thought she stayed single because nobody interested her, or that she was into Tyler, but he'd turned her down or some shit. A lie I told myself to feel better, really, as I knew deep down Tyler would never turn her down if given the chance.

'You've kissed other guys,' I pointed out. 'Fuck, Ari, you

stayed out in the pool house last night with a complete stranger! The whole reason we're even having this conversation.'

'You haven't even asked if we did anything. There's no way for you to know whether we kissed or had sex or whatever! You're assuming and thinking the worst of me, right?' Her face crumbled. 'And you know what hurts the most? How little you think of me. That you can go around fucking Savannah like there's no issue, and I'm to stay a celibate nun just in case. That's what hurts the most, Rock.'

When my dad left, I thought I would never feel worse than I did in that moment. Clearly, I was young, foolish, and oh so very wrong.

Because the hurt in her eyes and the vitriol in her words hurt more than anything else I'd ever experienced.

'Ari, I—'

'No.' She shook her head, her ponytail once more unstuck and swinging along with her. 'I don't want to hear it. You need to take a good look at yourself before we spend time together. I can't be around you if you're still with her.'

'I'm sorry,' I whispered, brushing a loose strand of her hair behind her ear. 'I really fucking am.'

'I know,' she replied. 'But this is one of those times where sorry isn't enough.'

Arianna didn't believe in grovelling. It was one of her least favourite parts of the films we watched and the books she read, so the fact she wasn't accepting my apology without any strings attached or any actions was what hurt *me* the most. In the past, sorry was always enough for her—as long as it was genuine and you didn't repeat whatever you were repenting for.

'What would be enough?'

'If I tell you, then it isn't real,' she whispered, blinking her tear-filled eyes. 'And I want it to be real.'

'Tell me what to do.'

'I can't,' she said, a tear finally falling. 'You need to do it yourself.'

With that, she moved back to the kitchen counter and picked up her phone, ready to order our food.

'Go pick a film, yeah?' she said, as if none of what just happened took place. 'I'll meet you in the cinema room once I've ordered.'

'Ari?'

'No.' Her red-rimmed eyes cut through mine. 'Tonight, we're the same as always. I sit on one sofa, you on another. We eat. We laugh. We watch a movie. That's it, Rock. That's all I can give you right now, and you shouldn't even be asking me for any more than that.'

'I'm sorry.'

'I know.'

Twenty-five

Arianna

age 18, march

HOW DID I always find myself in such stupid situations?

Honestly, it was a question I asked myself on the daily. And even after asking myself daily, I still didn't have a valid fucking answer.

'Do you think I should call her?'

'Call who?'

If he mentions her name again, I may scream.

I turned to face Gray, who had manoeuvred us on the sofa until I was sitting on his lap, draped my arm around his shoulder, and pulled a face. If he'd pulled me onto his lap, it meant he wanted to talk about something without others overhearing.

So far, I'd only spotted a couple of guys from school, Alex and Peter, who were friends with one of Gray's old mates Dean Walters. I didn't mention it to Gray as he looked lost in thought, but Dean was in a relationship with Beth's best friend, Layla, meaning they'd probably be spreading around what they'd seen and causing aggro.

People never seemed to understand that Gray and I were friends and just that. There'd never been anything between us like that, and I imagined that kissing him would be like kissing an uncle I didn't want to go near or something.

Plus, it wasn't like I'd been sitting on his lap the whole night. We'd been sitting next to each other on the sofa for ages, talking about everything and nothing while we drank away our sorrows, while ignoring the surrounding party for the most part.

'JACOBS!' he shouted over the loud bass playing through the speakers in the tiny living room we were in. Somebody Gray knew was throwing a house party, and of course that meant I had to go with him as his buddy. 'Should I call Jacobs?'

'Why would you do that?' I asked, bored already. Ever since the girl started at Hollowdale, he hadn't shut up about her and ever since I'd heard about him going upstairs with her at his birthday party, I'd known something had gone down between them. He just hadn't told me yet.

'To talk to her.' He ran his hand through his hair, his azure eyes looking into mine, wanting to see something I wasn't giving. 'See how she's doing.'

I stayed quiet, waiting for him to get the rest of whatever it was off his chest.

He hadn't brought her up for no reason.

'Did I tell you she's my girlfriend?' he asked, and for the first time in a while, the boy had managed to surprise the shit out of me.

'Your girlfriend?' I asked, stumped. 'Since when?'

'Since I passed that science test and we went for dessert. She looked so cute and so down that day that I couldn't help but ask her. I know you've not spent much time with her, or us, but she's really cool, Ree, and I think the two of you will get on loads.'

'Then why don't you invite her out with us or something? Shit, dude, you didn't even tell me you're together.'

'Feeling a little hurt?' he asked, and although his tone was teasing, he was being serious. Gray never wanted to hurt me; never wanted me to feel second-best or like I wasn't worthy of love and affection. I nodded, feeling vulnerable and uncomfortable because of it. 'Time for a hug.'

I put my arms around Gray's neck and leaned down,

hugging him to me, happy he wasn't anywhere near as drunk as usual. My lips went to his ear. 'I'm happy if you're happy, Gray. You deserve someone who loves you for you.'

'Who said anything about love?'

'You know what I mean,' I said, pulling back and pushing his shoulder with a little more force than intended. 'I'm happy for you both, seriously.'

'Well, if we're talking about people who deserve someone who loves them…'

'Don't even go there,' I warned, knowing I didn't want to hear the next sentence. Because we'd been here before. It wasn't the first time I'd shown up at the rodeo to find it was a Rock Rodeo. And for those uninformed, a Rock Rodeo was basically a way for Gray—or Tyler—to convince me to get my head out of my arse and approach Rock to tell him how I felt about him. Or something along those lines. Each time they tried, I shut them down pretty effectively within a half hour. 'I thought we agreed we weren't going to talk about him tonight.'

'Well, I lied.' Gray shrugged. 'You need to talk about it.'

'I don't.'

'Fine! You *should* talk about it then because it's only sitting in the back of your mind and festering.'

'Since when did you turn into a shrink?'

'Since when did you back down from being a badass?'

'This has nothing to do with being badass, Gray. It has to do with me not wanting to talk about a stupid dickhead who has a girlfriend!'

'A girlfriend he doesn't like as much as he likes you.'

'So why is he with her then?' I asked, frustrated the same way I was every time we had the same conversation. The same conversation we had at least once a month—minimum.

'Because you're a silly twat who pushed him away after giving him your V-card!' Gray chuckled, and I couldn't get mad at him when all he did was speak the truth. 'That boy was willing to say fuck it to your parents and you didn't even give him the time of day.'

'He went and found Savannah soon enough!'

'Because he's also a silly twat.'

I shook my head and removed myself from Gray's grip, needing to put distance between us.

'Can we go?'

Gray stood and followed me out of the house, but not before grabbing a beer for the road.

Once outside, I stomped to my car, hoping he was still following. The wind blew my hair in front of my face, and I was fighting with it when Gray came and got in the unlocked car. 'You getting in, Ree, or what?'

'Sort of fighting with the wind here!'

'Funny enough, there's no wind in the car. Get in.'

I didn't want to point out once in the car that the boy was right. Of course there was no wind in there. I shook my head and swivelled my mirror to rearrange my hair into something that didn't resemble a bird's nest.

'I kissed him,' I said, keeping my eyes on my own in the mirror, not wanting to see Gray's reaction, but sensing it regardless.

'Kissed *who*?'

'Rock, of course. Who did you think I meant?'

'Well, you have been known to kiss Tyler…'

My elbow jutted out, catching him on the side of the face.

'Ouch!'

'You make it sound like I'm a little kiss slut!'

'No…' he trailed off, not looking in my direction. 'Nothing like that. It's just—'

'It's just, what?' I bit out through gritted teeth.

'Well, have you spoken to Tyler about all that went down between the two of you?'

'Nothing went down between the two of us,' I stressed, but the way my stomach bottomed out told me I knew I wasn't completely telling the whole truth. 'Okay, nothing *major* went down between us.'

'But have you spoken to him?'

'No, but—'

'Ree, there's no but about it.'

Why the fuck is Gray the person speaking the truth right now?

'Fine! I need to talk to him.'

'Now.'

'Now?'

'Now! Put the car into drive and head over to Ty's flat, pronto.'

Without another word, I did as Gray said, but I wasn't happy about it.

GRAY STAYED IN THE CAR.

So, there I was, standing outside Tyler's door, the rain beginning to pour, unsure how the fuck I'd let Gray talk me into coming to talk to Ty. The main reason I'd been putting it off? I didn't really know what to say to him. What was there to say? *I'm sorry I kissed you, multiple times, even though we both know I like somebody else.*

I took a deep breath and rapped on the door.

Within a moment, the door opened to reveal Tyler standing there, his dark brown hair wet from the shower. Then my eyes tracked downwards... to the towel wrapped around his waist— and nothing else.

'Princess,' he said, his eyes widening when he took in my appearance. 'What're you doing here?'

'Can I come in?'

He stepped away, allowing me entrance, and I went inside without looking back at my car, or Gray sat inside it.

Without being told, I made my way inside Ty's place to his living room and sat down on the sofa with a large thud, practically throwing myself against the cushions.

Ty had lived in the flat ever since we started year twelve and it was one of the Rebels' hangout spots aside from the field. It was owned by his parents and once he turned seventeen, they decided he could live there without them as they wanted their house all to themselves.

'You okay?' he asked, coming to join me in the room, sitting in the armchair opposite me. 'You come here alone?'

'Gray's in the car,' I said before realising that maybe I shouldn't have told him that. If Gray had stayed in the car, then it was clear I wasn't sticking around long. 'No doubt he's about to call Jacobs or something.'

'That new girl he likes?'

'Yep. He's a little smitten with her.'

'I saw them go to your spare room the night of Gray's party.'

'Yeah, Rock mentioned that Savannah saw them, too.'

'As long as he's happy, right?'

'Of course,' I said with a nod, swallowing down my discomfort. 'So… Can I be honest?'

'You can always be honest with me, princess.'

'Right.' The discomfort grew. 'So, the truth is I'm here under duress.'

'Because of Grayson?'

'Well, besides you, he's the only other person who could force me to do shit.'

'True, true.' He leaned forward, his eyes searching my face. 'So, why's Gray forced you here?'

'He wants me to talk to you about our… kisses. Clear a few things up, I suppose.' I shrugged. Maybe if I acted nonchalant enough, I'd start to believe my own indifference.

'We haven't kissed since the field party at the start of school. That was months ago.'

'I know that.'

'And we spoke about it afterwards.'

'I know that too.'

'So?'

'Gray doesn't know about those talks, and I guess he's looking out for us both. Or maybe he's meddling in our lives so I don't go and meddle in his?' I shrugged. 'No idea.'

Tyler smiled, a mischievous look covering his face.

'Well, come on then, princess. Say the words you've been forced to come here and say.'

He was teasing me, and I was going to let him.

Ever since the first time we kissed at a field party a couple of years ago, I never wanted our friendship to change. Never wanted things to become serious, or one-sided, or literally anything that would stop us from remaining the best of friends.

'So… I kissed Rock.'

'You did, huh?' The look on his face wasn't surprised enough for him to not have seen it coming. 'And are we only talking about the kiss yesterday?'

'You know about the one last night?'

'I didn't.' He shrugged. 'But, Ari, he was so angry when you didn't come home and worried for you that I knew the time where he'd say fuck it wasn't too far off.'

'Oh.'

'He texted me when he couldn't find you. He was freaking out, worried that stranger you'd disappeared with had taken you somewhere or something, and nobody could even tell him the name of the dude.'

'Neither could I,' I admitted, wincing at the foolishness of it all. 'He never told me his name.'

'I'm not gonna tell you how dumb that was 'cause I have a feeling you know that already.'

I nodded, not needing a lecture from him—there was nothing he could say to me that I hadn't already said to myself.

'Princess,' he said, rubbing his jaw before connecting our gazes, 'all I've ever wanted is for you and Rock to sort it out.

Ever since that first kiss when I suggested we make him jealous, that's all I've wanted for you. Did things get twisted somewhere along the line? Sure, but we both knew the score. So, before you think about apologising to me or some other stupid shit like that, don't. We're still best friends, no matter what happens between you and doucheface.'

'You like Rock,' is all I could think to say.

'Yeah, I do. Which is why I'm happy the two of you are figuring it out.'

'He still has a girlfriend,' I pointed out.

'Doubt he will for much longer,' Tyler said. 'Especially if you've kissed him.'

'Technically, he kissed me.'

'And we're running on technicalities now, are we, princess?'

'Yep,' I said with a shrug. 'Pretty much.'

I looked down at my phone, to the text Rock had sent me an hour or so before, and I read it for maybe the fiftieth time. I knew I should do as he asked, or at least reply to him, but I hadn't moved to do either.

> Please come home when you read this. I've got something urgent I want to talk to you about.

'You gonna put the boy out of his misery?' Ty asked, nudging his head in my phone's direction, looking at the message displayed.

'Maybe later.'

He nodded. 'I've got your back no matter what, princess.'

I smiled, knowing he meant it and that everything was good between us. 'I know.'

Twenty-Six

Arianna

age 18, march

WHEN I GOT HOME after the party with Gray and visiting Tyler, I'd attempted to enter the house in silence, not wanting to alert anybody to my presence. Gray and I ended up staying over at Ty's and having a quick nap, because it was already five in the morning by the time Ty and I stopped talking.

So locking eyes with Rock the moment I walked through the door definitely wasn't in my plan. Especially not so soon after admitting to my two closest friends that we'd kissed.

'Trying to sneak in?' he growled, crossing his arms across his chest, and I couldn't help but focus on the way his muscles strained with the motion.

Like a child caught out, the only thing I thought to do was open my mouth and say, 'Err…'

Real helpful, Ari.

'I texted you last night,' Rock said, taking a step back so I could reach the stairs without colliding with him. 'I expected you to come home.'

'Oh? So, because you texted me, I was supposed to just rush home? As if a summoning is enough for me to drop my own plans? Seriously, Rock. I thought you were better than that.'

'But I've got news.'

'News that demanded I be home within seconds?' I made a sound low in my throat, pissed he was acting like such a prick at nine in the morning. 'What did you want to talk to me about?'

'Can we go somewhere a little more… private?' He looked around the hallway with shifting eyes, but there was nobody there.

'If you insist.' I knew he was getting frustrated with my (mostly fake) nonchalance, but I didn't give a fuck. He should know that I wasn't the person you summoned like a person who didn't matter.

Rock walked up the stairs at a crawling pace, ensuring I was following him every few steps, as if worried I would flitter away when he wasn't looking—and a part of me had considered fleeing, but the small slither of my brain that wanted to know why he'd wanted me home so bad won out.

He continued until he entered his bedroom before stopping inside by his bed. The door slammed behind me, making me jump, and then when I realised we were alone together without anybody else around, I shied away from him.

The tension, the chemistry, all of it, that lingered between us was always more pronounced once alone. It was why I'd avoided being alone with him, especially since he asked Savannah to be his girlfriend—even if he'd asked her because I'd basically forced him into a corner.

'So…'

'So…' he repeated, searing me with his gaze until I felt way too hot and bothered for so early in the morning after such a long night.

'What did you want me home for?'

'I wanted to talk to you.'

'And you couldn't wait until this morning?'

'I was feeling a little on edge,' he admitted, looking a little shifty, averting his eyes from perusing my face. 'I didn't want you to hear it from anyone but me.'

'Hear what?'

'I ended things with Savannah.'

My heart stuttered in my chest, unsure if it was hearing him correctly. Ever since he asked Savannah out, I'd written Rock off to a degree. Clearly, he didn't want to fight for me after I told him to find somebody else. Fuck, the boy didn't even wait longer than a day to do just that.

Over the past year and the handful of months since that September weekend, I'd reconciled with it in my mind, knowing that he did what he thought was best at the time. I couldn't hate him for his stupidity—not like he could help it.

'You what?'

'Ended things with Sav—'

'I heard you,' I blurted out.

'Then why'd you ask me to repeat it?'

'You're such a guy, Rock,' I scoffed, rolling my eyes at his literal thinking. If there was ever a prize handed out for a literal thinker, Rock would be the winning recipient, that was for sure. 'I just… never mind.'

'I wanted you to be the first to know.'

'Thanks?' Did he think he was doing me a favour or something? Like of course I was thrilled inside that he'd ended things, but him ending something he should've ended a *long* time ago wasn't going to have me break out into dance or anything.

'What's up?'

'Nothing. I just don't know what you want from me here. Like thanks for doing something you shoulda done weeks, fuck, months ago? Ultimately, I can't control your life or your actions.'

'I realised how much of a prick I was being and I couldn't do it any longer.'

'How noble of you.'

'Ice queen,' he said, somehow making his nickname for me sound like a plea, 'I'm trying here.'

'I can see that, but I don't quite understand *why*.'

'What do you mean?'

'What do you want from me?' I caught myself and how loud

my voice was before continuing. No idea if Dad and Gigi were home or not, but I didn't want them to come barging in while we were having a long overdue conversation. 'What do you expect me to do? Did you think I'd waltz in here, you'd tell me you're single now, and I'd just launch myself into your arms like some crappy rom-com?'

'No, I—'

'Do you see the issue here?'

'I didn't,' he said with a small chuckle, 'but now that we're in the moment, I'm seeing the flaw in my thinking, yeah.'

My laughter joined his, awkward and slightly stilted, but I took a step closer to him nonetheless. He was like a magnet, pulling me in until I couldn't control my actions any longer.

'Ari,' he started, mirroring my step forward. 'I'm sorry. It's just ever since I ended it with her, I've wanted to speak to you, to tell you, and then when you didn't reply to my text or come home straight away, I became a defensive arsehole about it all.'

'I'm just gonna interject and say you need to sort that out. There's only so often I can overlook and accept that you're a massive wanker, you know?'

'I know.' His smile was crooked and fucking endearing, yet the wrinkles around his eyes told me he was fighting his emotions. Or maybe it was me who was fighting their emotions? 'And the fact you're even in the room with me right now is something I'm super stoked about.'

'Super stoked? How old are you?'

'Take the piss all you want,' he said, taking yet another small step closer. Soon he'd be towering over me, and I'd have to look up at his face. 'I'm not even going to take it back because I mean it. I'm always chuffed when you give me the time of day.'

'Now you're just trying to make me blush.'

'And succeeding.'

My fingers went to my cheeks involuntarily, as if I'd be able to feel the flush Rock said was covering my face, but of course I couldn't. My cheeks were a little warm but nothing major.

'Whatever.'

The air between us was filled with a tension I'd tried to ignore but couldn't any longer. As much as I didn't want to be the girl who kissed the guy the day after him ending things with his long-term girlfriend, it looked like I was indeed going to be that girl.

Should I make him grovel?

I knew a few people who believed I should, but that wasn't my style. I hated that girls found a grovelling man attractive.

Obviously, I wanted an apology. Who wouldn't?

But an apology, if meant and heartfelt, was more than enough for me.

'Ari,' he said, his eyes softening in my direction. 'I'm sorry, for a lot of things, but I'm especially sorry for not ending things with Savannah after what happened between us at Beurrefest this year. I was a wanker and I wanted you to hurt the way I hurt after the first time we slept together.'

I'd guessed that was why he'd acted the way he had, but to have him confirm it, without any lies or him trying to minimise his actions, helped the anger inside me to float away. We'd both made poor decisions when it came to each other after all.

'I accept your apology,' I said, blinking at him, my thoughts rushing around to try and think of something cohesive to say. 'And I'm sorry it's taken us this long to pull our heads out of our arses.'

He chuckled at that. 'And I know it's soon, and I shouldn't even be expecting this of you right now but now I'm single I need to ask you.'

'Ask me what?' My heart swooped and I knew we were on the edge of something. Something important that neither of us could brush off when we were doubting everything.

'Ari'—he took a deep breath, running his hand along his buzzed head—'will you be my girlfriend?'

'Yes,' I breathed out, the rightness of the moment overwhelming me. 'Of course.'

His eyes lit up, the gleam in them something both wicked and gentle at the same time. 'I'm going to kiss you now, if that's okay?'

'Since when have you ever *asked* to kiss me?' I laughed, our bodies touching now that he'd stepped closer once more. 'You're usually the guy who takes what he wants.'

'Oh yeah?' He tilted his head, just a little, and I smiled at the brightness lingering in his eyes. 'Maybe I should take what I want, then.'

My words came out in a hushed whisper. 'Maybe you should.'

TWENTY-SEVEN
ROCK

age 18, march

'Maybe you should,' she whispered.

And it was all I needed.

I took Ari's hand in mine, looking earnestly into her eyes, and smiled, ready for whatever was going to happen next.

My heart was pounding knowing we were on the cusp of something, and unlike the last time, I wouldn't let her talk me out of anything. Wouldn't let her slip through my fingers without putting up a fight.

Our lips collided in the kiss we'd both waited for a lot longer than we should've. We'd both done things we regretted, but that time was over with. No more regrets.

Releasing her, I reached behind her back and yanked the zipper of her dress down, though it got stuck halfway from the brutal treatment. 'Turn around.'

She did as I asked and I eased the zip all the way down before helping her step out of it.

'Go get on the bed,' I whispered in her ear, taking a step back so she could get around me before following closely behind her. A slight shiver ran down my spine as I watched her lie on the bed, awaiting further instruction. She was so beautiful it hurt.

I removed my clothing piece by piece, knowing Ari's eyes

were firmly on my every movement, and I rejoiced in the moment, enjoying her attention being fully on me with no distractions.

Once fully undressed, I closed the distance between us and went to kneel by her feet, perusing her body from head to toe. Taking in the slight flush covering her face, her breasts, before my eyes travelled further south.

My hands reached out to her thighs of their own accord, and it wasn't until I was pushing her thighs apart to allow myself access that I realised what I was doing and who I was doing it with.

Arianna. The girl I'd always wanted to make mine. The one who finally *was* mine.

'I can't get enough of you,' I told her, the awe I felt towards her evident in my voice. I kissed her legs, biting my way up until I was in between her thighs, my breath fanning across her pussy. 'This is even better than my imagination told me it would be.'

'Fantasised about this, have you?' she asked with a small chuckle, but when I looked up at her face, there wasn't a trace of humour there.

'Fuck yeah.'

A sharp squeak of surprise left her when my mouth descended on her at last, softly brushing over her clit. *Ah, shit.* Even that slight swipe told me she tasted even better than in my fantasies.

My tongue didn't stay soft for long, my mouth quickly devouring her, licking and nipping at every part available to me, wanting to dig, search, and investigate every inch of skin. *Very* sensitive skin, if her small moans were anything to go by. All they did was encourage me to keep going, fully burying myself between her legs.

It didn't take long before Ari was unable to control the sounds coming from her lips, her legs shaking as they instinctively tried to clamp down on my head, seemingly wanting to keep me there forever. Hell, I wasn't going to complain if she did. It was too damn good.

When my fingers dug into her ass to keep her still, pulling her even harder against my mouth, she began to whimper and it turned me the fuck on. Even more than her scent. Her taste.

Just her in general.

Her pants increased, and I knew she was close to falling over the edge. I slipped a finger inside her to help her along, and that was when she clamped my head and screamed. 'Rock!'

Once she loosened her legs and let my head free, I moved back onto my knees and climbed over her to place a firm kiss on her lips.

'You are amazing,' I said against her mouth. 'Why has it taken us so long to get to this point again?'

'Because I was an arse. And then you were an arse. A vicious cycle if there ever was one.'

'At least you can admit it,' I said, chuckling. As much as I wanted to have sex with her right then and there, I didn't want to ruin the moment and make it seem as if that was all I wanted from her. Of course I wanted to sleep with her, but I also didn't want her to think that was all I wanted. Then an idea struck me. 'We could take this to the bathroom?'

I doubted she'd say yes, so shock ran through me when she softened, chuckling. 'And do what, exactly?'

I raised my eyebrows at her suggestively, hunger stirring in my belly as I pictured myself pressed up against her in the shower.

'Surely your mind can come up with something we can do?'

'You just want to see me naked.'

'You're already naked,' I pointed out and we both chuckled. 'We both need to shower, but I'm not ready for your scent to be gone, so the shower it is.'

'The logic isn't holding up.'

'Are you trying to *stop* us from showering together?'

She pursed her lips before shaking her head with vigour. 'Show me what you can do.'

Leaning into our shared shower, Arianna turned on the water, letting it warm up before getting in. For years we'd shared a bathroom, and every time I knew Arianna was in the shower, I'd restrained myself. Not that I'd ever tried to enter without her knowing or anything, but the thoughts of her in there were enough to send me over the edge. I may have jerked myself to the image of her in there… more than once.

As she leaned in, her perfect round arse was in my view, and I nearly came again at the sight of her. Giving it a slap, I growled instructions in her ear to get into the shower and let me have my way with her. I didn't want to wait anymore now that things were becoming reality between us.

She shivered lightly against me before obeying, clambering into the shower. Once the water was running down her body, I joined her, glad for once that we didn't have a huge shower so there was nowhere for me to go but up against her skin.

Her body was still as she faced me, anticipation and curiosity on her face as she watched my every movement. I pressed a firm kiss to her lips as I reached past her for her shampoo, then continued devouring her lips and tongue as I popped it open and poured a small blob onto her head, already soaked from the hot water pouring down.

Quickly manoeuvring her out of the stream of water, I ended the kiss, my lips begging for more of her as I got to work washing her hair. The delayed gratification would only make it better for both of us, and it was best we both cooled down before we went again, so I did my best to ignore my hunger for the woman pressed against me, focusing on my fingers instead. I still couldn't believe we were finally in our shower together after all this time.

Once her scalp had been thoroughly massaged, the shampoo worked up into a thick lather, I spun her around again, plunging her beneath the water. Ari let out a tiny gasp and I chuckled at the look on her face. The tiny sound only increased my hunger for her, the smallest reminder of the noises she'd made in my bed enough to set me on edge, reminding me of how desperately I needed to hear them again—and soon.

Shoving those thoughts down as my cock rose, I roughly grabbed the body scrubber and body wash, again switching places with Ari. 'Turn around,' I growled out.

She followed my instruction wordlessly and I stepped forward, coming closer, coming up against her until my cock was pressed firmly in between her arse cheeks.

How am I going to survive having a girlfriend with such a perfect body? I could barely survive when she wasn't mine.

I started cleaning her shoulders, slowly sweeping across her collarbone, then down each arm before moving to her breasts. I circled around them first, ensuring everything was coated in soap before moving my gentle attention to her nipples, already gathered into stiff peaks that had me aching to tug at them with my teeth. Instead, I played with them softly with my other hand, amazed at how soft and smooth they felt with the soap.

I continued as I washed the rest of her, as she leaned back into me, soft moans of enjoyment coming from her lips that nearly sent me over the edge prematurely.

As much as I couldn't wait to go rough with her, I found myself enjoying the slow tease as well. It was a different kind of appreciation of her body.

I loved that I was finally able to feel her move so slowly against me, to finally have her in my arms, in my heart.

I couldn't wait any longer. I had to touch her. Had to hear her tiny moans as she climaxed. I stopped washing her body, and my hands travelled downwards, spreading her thighs apart. My fingers reached between her folds and brushed up against her clit, finding it with instinctive precision. Arianna was wet and wanting, and it made my dick harden to the point of pain as she arched against me, panting with need. *Fuck.*

'Fuck,' Ari groaned, riding my hand as desperate for me as I was for her, arching against me as one hand reached back to grip the back of my head, pulling me closer.

I bit her earlobe and pulled her into the water with me. 'Shit, I need you to finish on my hand. I need to feel you fall apart while I hold you up. I want you to scream, baby.'

Her pleasure mounted faster with each word I spoke and it made me smug as shit. Finally, with a loud shout of my name, Ari let out her release, her legs shaking, barely able to hold her up, all while trembling in my arms.

I didn't give her long to recover, moving her against the wall of the shower until her tits were pressed to it, her head turned to look at me, dazed but still filled with a hunger I knew was reflected in my own eyes.

'Fuck me, Ari, you're too damn sexy for your own good,' I growled, pushing my cock inside her. She was already slick from her recent orgasm, her walls tight with need, and it was a damn good thing I knew how to hold myself off, or I would have finished in just a few pumps. Ari was everything I'd always wanted, and the reality was much better than my dreams.

As I moved inside her, awed at how amazing she felt on my cock, my mind wandered back to our first time together and how different this evening was to that. We'd grown up, sure, but there was more to it than that. This time we were coming together as a couple—as two people who were willing to fight to be together no matter the repercussions of our actions.

She whimpered, a wordless beg for more; for me to give her another release. *This girl is all mine,* I thought to myself in disbelief, grabbing her hips to pull her tighter against me.

The sounds of her enjoyment increased the faster I moved, the harder I thrust, as my breath came out in short, controlled bursts as I did my best to bring her to climax before I got there myself.

Teetering on the edge, not willing to go over before Ari did, I kept going, wanting her to feel the way I did.

'Fuck, Rock,' Ari shouted, and I knew she was close. More

moans and words left her lips as she seemed to plunge headfirst into her orgasm.

Her walls clenched around me so hard I wouldn't have been able to fight off my own orgasm if I tried. Grunting, my body released its load, pulsing for longer than I had anything to give.

That was… fucking amazing.

I felt light-headed from the intensity, but I wasn't about to leave it at that without letting her know how much I loved and worshipped her.

Flipping Arianna around to face me, I put my forehead on hers, catching my breath for a moment before kissing her adoringly, my hands resting on her waist. She kissed me back with as much enthusiasm and I knew she was my forever from that one kiss alone.

There was nothing that could stop us, and there was no way I was letting her go ever again.

I couldn't do this life without her.

TWENTY-EIGHT
ROCK

age 18, march

AFTER WE CLEANED UP, the two of us went back to my room and got comfortable in my bed.

It was something I'd dreamed of for a long time, and fuck me, it was even better than I'd ever imagined it would be to have her curled up beside me naked, perfectly fitting in the spot in front of me, her back pressed up against my chest like she'd been made to fit right there.

'I suppose we should talk,' she said, a little laugh vibrating her body.

'What about?' I asked, not wanting to needle her if she wasn't ready for it, even though she was the one who'd suggested we talk.

'Not sure exactly,' she replied. 'Tyler and Savannah might be a good place to start.'

'And you want to have this conversation while facing away from me?'

'Oh, one thousand percent,' she said, and I laughed at her tone. 'I'm more likely to find it easier to be honest while staring at your bedroom wall.'

'If you insist.'

'I do.'

'Shall I start?' I asked, knowing the first thing I wanted to say was on the tip of my tongue—I also knew Arianna may have suggested we talk, but that she'd find it hard to actually start. She nodded, so I said, 'Back at Beurrefest the first time, all weekend I'd been building myself up to get you alone. It was all I wanted and I'd concocted ways for it to happen without it seeming too contrived or whatever.' I laughed. 'And then finally there we were, together, alone, in a tent.'

She stayed quiet, but it wasn't an uncomfortable silence.

'And we had sex, and it was fucking perfect, you know? I thought that was it. That we were on the same page and everything was gonna be hunky dory from then on. But maybe I should've spoken to you about it *before* we had sex, and not just assumed. Things would've gone a little different if I had.'

'I'm at fault too,' she butted in, not letting me take the complete blame. 'I also assumed we were on the same page about it being something we both wanted, but also knowing it was something that couldn't *go* anywhere.'

'We're both stupid, but either way, it happened and you rejected me, and I couldn't handle it. It had taken me so long to gain the courage to kiss you, and show you how I felt, that when you said you didn't want me, I just went into self-destruct mode within hours.

'Then you went off with the guys to see Dagger and I just didn't want to be around you. I stayed behind drinking, as you know, and that was how I met Savannah.' I shrugged—or at least I shrugged with the shoulder that wasn't resting on my mattress —not having much else to say to justify my shit, but knowing I needed to try anyway. 'And she listened to me.'

'You're the one who asked her out after a couple of hours.' Her voice was barely above a whisper and I could hear the hurt there.

'I didn't.' I heard her take a deep breath to interrupt, so I continued before she could stop my flow of thought. 'I just said it when you all came back, never expecting her to go along with it. Or at least I thought she'd nod along, and then tell me to fuck off afterwards. But as we both know, that isn't what went down.'

'So how did you end up *actually* becoming a couple?'

'She was gonna be new to school, and I sort of persuaded her to give me a chance so she wouldn't be starting a new school with no friends.' I laughed, hearing it for the first time and seeing it for what it was. 'I suppose at first we were both using each other, but only one of us knew that we were. Then after a while, it just sort of became… real.'

'That's sort of what happened with me and Tyler,' she whispered, turning to lay on her back and stare up at the ceiling. I moved and did the same, taking her hand in mine to squeeze it in solidarity. To let her know I was there and listening to her. No matter what she was about to say. 'At first, we kissed to make you jealous. It was Ty's idea, and I went along with it, thinking it couldn't hurt. Then when it actually worked and it seemed to rile you up, it only made sense to keep going.'

'Do you have feelings for him?' I had to know.

'Ones of friendship, sure, but nothing romantic. We started it all as a way to forget our own shit and it worked. Maybe a little too well, because the moment you thought I was into Tyler, you may have got jealous, but you also backed off too in a way. Threw yourself harder into your relationship with Savannah.'

'I'm sorry for rejecting you after we had sex at the festival this time around,' I said, needing her to know how much I regretted my bullshit actions. 'I wanted you to feel the way I had the year before.'

She gripped my hand tighter, sending support through our connection.

'But I also knew I was being a wanker because I had a girl-friend and I *still* didn't end things with her afterwards.'

'That was very wanker-ish of you,' she agreed, a smile in her voice. 'But I'm glad we've both come to terms with our shitty actions. I accept your apology, anyway.'

I wanted to tell her I loved her, but the moment was a little too raw. Too soon.

The fact she'd agreed to be my girlfriend was enough to keep me going and I thought if I opened up too much, too fast, she'd bolt scared.

'I'm sorry too,' she said, letting a breath out. 'I've had a crush on you since way before we came stepsiblings, but I never thought I could tell you, and then all of a sudden our parents were married and you were completely off-limits no matter how I felt towards you. I've never wanted to disappoint my dad and I know how close you and your mum are.' She reached up with her free hand and wiped away a tear from under her eye. I wanted to kiss her tears away, but it wasn't the time. Ari opening up was something to cherish and I didn't want to scare her. 'I thought our timing was always going to be off.'

'I did too,' I admitted. 'But I hoped I was wrong.'

She chuckled. 'And of course you were the right one out of the two of us.'

'Always, babe.' I turned my head to kiss her on the cheek, tasting the saltiness of her tears, before laying back again. 'Thank fuck our timing is finally right.'

Ari's sniffles made me smile. Everything was finally going our way and I couldn't be happier.

My phone buzzed from where I'd left it underneath my pillow and I winced, hoping I wasn't about to open my phone to a message from Savannah asking me to reconsider.

But it wasn't Savannah.

If anything, it was even worse than that.

> Mother - Can't wait to see you tomorrow! Tony and I will be home before dinner as we have important guests coming. Make sure you and Ari are dressed appropriately! Love you lots baby boy x

And just like that, we both came down to earth with a bang.

Talk about off timing.

Our parents arrived home later that night with fanfare.

The two of them were beyond thrilled to be home, beyond thrilled to see their children again, and beyond thrilled to have staff who knew them inside and out.

Or so my mum said once she swanned through the door.

All morning, Ari and I made sure to sneak in as many kisses —and orgasms—as we could before our parents came home and ruined our newfound fun.

Arianna looked stunning, dressed in a beautiful black dress that showed off every luscious curve, and all I wanted to do was touch her, but since our parents were home, she was once more off-limits.

Even if she was my girlfriend.

Fuck. I still couldn't believe that somehow, she was my girl. That the person I'd wanted all this time was now somebody I could touch and kiss whenever I wanted—well, as long as the 'rents were out of the way. Thank heaven they spent so much time away on holidays.

I was one lucky fucker.

'You look amazing,' I told her, my eyes falling to the low neckline of her dress, and wishing I had a view of what was below it. 'Shame we have to attend this dinner.'

'Why's that?'

'Because I really want to see you *out* of it.'

'That can be arranged,' she said, a saucy look on her face. I reached out to take her in my arms but stopped the moment I saw our parents enter the hallway.

'Hey, you two,' Tony said. 'Thanks for holding down the fort while we've been gone!'

'It was nothing,' I replied because it really wasn't. There was staff around at all times to cater to us, and it wasn't like Ari and I were cleaning the place or anything. Half the time we forgot they were even supposed to live here. 'We're just glad the two of you had the best time.'

'Oh, it really was the best,' Mum said, sauntering over to give me a big hug. 'It always is, but as always, I missed you so much.'

'I missed you too, Mum,' I murmured back. Our relationship had changed ever since she became Mrs Hollowdale, but that was to be expected, especially as I got older and we spent less time together. But I always felt a lot better whenever she was home. Like a piece of me, tiny but important, was missing when she was gone.

'I can't wait to hear all about what I've missed,' she said, putting her hand in the crook of my arm, ready to walk into dinner together. 'And don't you two give us the runaround that you've not been up to much. We speak to the staff. We know what goes on here.'

I coughed and saw Ari's face go the colour of her hair. 'Hopefully, not *all* that goes on. There's only so much I want my mother to know.'

Mum tittered as if I'd told the world's funniest joke and not something I actually meant, but that was my mum for you. Never taking anything too seriously.

'You look beautiful,' Tony told Ari and she gave him a thin-lipped smile in return. 'Thank you for making an effort tonight. I'm extremely lucky to have you as my daughter.'

'Thanks, Dad,' she mumbled, her face going an even darker shade of red. If she kept blushing, you wouldn't be able to decipher where her face ended and her hair began.

Ari put her hand in the crook of her father's arm and the four of us entered the dining room.

'Our guests are on their way,' Tony said once we were all seated. I was sitting with Ari on my right, and an empty seat was beside her. Opposite me was Tony, then my mother sat opposite

Arianna, with an empty seat to her left. Looked like two people were joining us then.

'Who are they?' I asked. The noise of pouring liquid filled the air as the staff filled our water glasses before returning with the wine. One thing I liked about Tony was he'd never treated either of us like kids. Ever since I became his stepson, we'd been allowed wine at dinner and other small perks like that. Our parents trusted us, and that was a hard pill to swallow—especially when Arianna and I weren't the most trustworthy when it came to telling them the truth.

'Harold and Harrison Baker, father and son,' he said, rubbing his large stomach. 'New to the area and extremely important men within their own right. Harrison is your age, too, so that's a plus.'

'We look forward to meeting them,' I said because it was expected of me, not because it was genuine. Plus, it meant Ari didn't have to speak, and that was always a good thing. She wasn't very good at being... tactful in certain situations. Or in any situations really.

It wasn't long before they were ushered in by the head house-keeper, a friendly gentleman named Mr Billins.

But it wasn't the two men who caught my attention.

It was the gasp that came from the girl to my right and the way her face paled, like a ghost had appeared at the table. A ghost she knew and was familiar with.

'Harold,' Tony greeted, standing to give the older man a firm handshake. We all stood when Tony did, not wanting to seem rude. 'You've met my wife, Gigi, but please meet my daughter Arianna and my stepson Rock. Arianna, Rock, this is Harold Baker. And next to him is his son Harrison.'

'Nice to meet you both,' said Harold.

Harrison smirked, his eyes alight with amusement. 'Nice to meet you, Rock.'

I nodded in greeting, in the way guys do, and waited for him to greet Ari so we could sit down again. My stomach rumbled and it wouldn't be long until it was loud enough for everybody to hear. A growing lad like me needed to eat—all the time.

'Arianna and I have met,' Harrison said, smiling at her with a secret smile I didn't appreciate him giving to my girlfriend. 'How are you doing, Ari?'

'I'm okay, thanks.' She averted her gaze, unable to look at him.

What the fuck?

'That's great!' Tony said, taking his seat, and we all followed suit. 'How did the two of you meet?'

'A party,' Harrison replied with a smugness I wanted to swipe away. 'Back in February.'

Shit. Fuck. Shit!

Harrison Baker was the mystery guy from that night?

Just when things were looking up for me and Ari, something just had to come along and bite us both on the arse. Of course it did.

We'd never exactly had much luck, had we?

Twenty-Nine

Arianna

age 18, march

EVER SINCE THE Bakers walked into the room, I felt like I'd entered a dream.

A very fucking bad dream.

A nightmare of epic proportions, if you will.

Under the table, a hand touched my thigh and gripped me in what I supposed was meant to be a comforting gesture, but really, it just made me feel even worse. Especially when I realised it was on my right thigh and not my left, meaning it wasn't Rock trying to comfort me.

Out of the side of my mouth, I whispered, 'After dinner's done, I want to talk to you.'

To his credit, *Harrison* didn't say anything, or even show any outward sign that I'd spoken at all, except a slight, almost imperceptible nod.

'I'm so glad you could join us,' my dad said, smarmy as all get-out. 'I was just telling my wife about the new contract.'

'Ah,' Harold said, getting comfortable in his chair as he spilled out on either side. 'Let's not talk business at the dinner table, Tony.'

'And there was me thinking that this entire dinner was because of business,' my dad said with a smug smile on his face and my insides soured. Nothing good ever came from my dad making that particular face. Pretty sure the last time I saw it was when he told me he was marrying Gigi and look how well that all worked out for me.

'All in good time, my man. All in good time.'

Once we were all seated, the staff came around and filled our wineglasses, and before they'd even moved on to Harrison, I had my glass in my hand and tilted to my lips.

There was no way I was getting through the dinner sober.

AFTER THE FIRST few courses were devoured, I settled in my seat a little.

Clearly, the ominous feeling that hit me when the Bakers entered the room was just hunger, or anxiety, or a little bit of both.

'Now that we've eaten,' my dad announced, silencing everybody at the table, 'and people have had time to get to know one another'—he glanced between me and Harrison, his eyes bugging out of his full face—'I'm happy for us to announce the news.'

'And who is "us"?' I asked, sceptical of what was to come next.

'Me and Harold here,' Dad said, nodding in the direction of the elder Baker. 'As you're all aware, business and family are two of the things that mean the most to me, and I've been a lucky man in that my business and family are something for me to be proud of.'

Rock squeezed my thigh underneath the table, his eyes still focused on the top of the table where my dad was now standing, having got to his feet during the opening of his speech.

'When I met Harold, we realised our core principles aligned

and that we could both benefit from doing business together…
amongst other things.'

'What Tony is trying to say,' Harold interjected, also rising to
stand, the stem of his wineglass gripped in his palm, 'is that
business is important, but what does business really mean if it
doesn't help your family? My family means everything to me,
and I couldn't be more honoured to find somebody who feels the
same way.'

What the fuck is going on?

'I can see from the looks on your faces that you're confused
and want me to get to the point. So, I shall. Tony and I have
come to an arrangement—one that will benefit all those who sit
around this table.' He smiled, and the only thought running
through my head was that if he smiled any wider, his lips would
split. 'I am here to announce the engagement of my son, Harrison, to Tony's daughter, Arianna.'

My mind went blank as I blinked, eyes on Harold, wondering
what the fuck was going on.

Surely, he didn't just say he was announcing an engagement
—*my* engagement? How could I be engaged without even
knowing about it? There had to be something I was missing…

Had I agreed to something when drunk that night at
Grayson's birthday party? No. I remembered everything that
took place between Harrison and me as I made sure not to get
too drunk. I never wanted to lose control of my actions, or
senses.

To my left, Rock's face was as confused as my own.

His stare was focused on Harold before he slowly moved it
along to my father, all the while blinking as if the view would
change if he only blinked enough to clear it.

'I—' Words failed me as my mouth opened and closed like a
guppy, unsure where to look or what to say next.

My head turned to Harrison, hoping to see the same disbelief
and confusion on his face, but that wasn't what I saw at all.

Nope.

Harrison looked, if anything, slightly smug?

Like he'd known coming into the dinner what was going to be announced and didn't mind it. That he even might *like* it.

What the fuck?

If I thought I needed to talk to him at the start of the meal, then I definitely needed to get him alone now. Sooner rather than later.

I opened my mouth to ask Harrison to come with me, but my dad began speaking first.

'I can see that we've blindsided you, my dear Arianna, but I promise you this is for the best. I would never make such a big decision for you if I didn't think it would bring you the ultimate happiness.' *And me the biggest financial gain,* being the words he left unsaid. Good old Dad, keeping it real as usual.

'Harrison,' I bit out, not wanting to react too harshly in front of everybody. My dad and I would be having words later, there was no doubt about that, but for the present, it was Harrison I needed to talk to the most.

Rock's eyes pleaded with me when I looked his way, but I couldn't give him anything—couldn't let people see the truth in our gazes—so I turned to Harrison instead.

'Can I talk to you in private?'

'Yes, yes!' my dad enthused, clapping his hands together. 'You two have much to discuss, I'm sure.'

Who the fuck is that man in front of me and what the hell did he do with my dad?

'Sure,' Harrison replied, his tone unaffected. 'I'd love to get to know you better, Arianna.'

My teeth were pressed so hard together I thought they were going to crack, but I gave a small, close-lipped smile.

'No need to rush back,' Harold said with a chortle. 'We'll all be here, ready to discuss further when you return.'

I stood, but Rock's hand around my wrist stopped me for a brief second, the look on his face nearly melting me. But I shook free from his grasp and kept my resolve.

'Let's go,' I said, turning to grab Harrison's hand to drag him along behind me. 'We've got a lot to talk about.'

He smiled and let me lead the way.

'DID YOU KNOW WHO I WAS?'

The moment the door slammed behind us, the words left me in a harsh whisper, not wanting anyone else in the house to over-hear us.

'At the party?' he asked, and I nodded. 'Of course. I told you I did, remember?'

I cast my mind back to that night and tried to recall the words he'd used to charm me.

'I think it's more exciting if I stay a mystery. You seem like the kind of girl who doesn't like mysteries.'

'And once again you're making an assumption about me, yet you know nothing about me.'

'I know this is your house. I know your name is Arianna.'

'Oh.'

Harrison laughed and the sound wasn't pleasant, but it also wasn't hideous either. Maybe learning a guy you hooked up with one random night was to be your fiancé in a few weeks' time was enough for everything they did to become sinister.

'Suppose this is why you didn't introduce yourself,' I grumbled.

'Wait a moment,' he said, placing his hand on my upper arm to stop my pacing. 'I knew who you were, sure. However, I didn't know our fathers' plans.'

'You expect me to believe that?'

'I do.' He nodded. 'Because it's the truth.'

'But you asked people about me at the party. You said so

yourself.' My accusation landed and his lips turned down, a brief flash of guilt, then gone before it settled.

'Okay, okay. So maybe my dad told me to meet you and introduce myself, but that's all. He never told me *why* he wanted me to do that, and to be frank with you, Arianna, I never asked. My father and I don't exactly have the kind of relationship where honesty is king.'

'Clearly, my father and I don't either,' I huffed out, pissed that my dad had ambushed me at dinner the way he had. The night before, he'd spoken to me, mentioned the upcoming dinner, and that was all—nothing about the fact he expected to sell me off like cattle.

'And let me guess. You're unhappy with the arrangement.'

'Aren't you?' I raised my voice and winced at how shrill I sounded. *This isn't me,* I thought, but there was no way to bring my heart rate down to a reasonable level, and therefore no way to stop my voice from coming out so unlike my own.

'I'm not unhappy,' Harrison admitted with a shrug. 'I'm also not thrilled about my choice being taken away from me.'

'But—'

'But,' he continued, as if I hadn't interrupted him, 'I don't dislike you, Arianna. I thought we hit it off at the party and I'd like to get to know you better before we do something drastic like disown ourselves from our families.'

'What are you saying?' *And why did it sound like he wasn't on my side?*

'I'm saying I'd like the two of us to date. Get to know one another properly now that everything is out in the open.'

'You're being serious, aren't you?'

'I'm not going to joke about something as serious as this. I've seen my dad deal with people who didn't make him happy— believe me, I'm not about to throw his plans away without putting in an effort first.'

'So, I'm just a pawn in games being played by old white men.'

'Pretty much.' Harrison chuckled, shaking his head at me, the pity he felt towards me shining in his dark eyes.

One of the things that was fucking me off the most?

The fact that I'd *liked* Handsome at the party. We had a good night together and had I not gone home to a pissed off Rock and a kiss that made my knees weak, I wouldn't be anywhere near as mad about the current situation I'd been thrown into. Not saying I'd have thanked my dad or anything, but I would've been more willing to get to know *Harrison* as himself and see how things went.

Somehow, even without knowing what was happening under his roof, my dad had managed to end my chance with Rock before it was allowed to begin.

It was as I'd said to Rock multiple times: *Our timing is off.*

And the sentence I'd never uttered after, but one that hung in the air like a bad smell: *I think it will always be off.*

'Look, Arianna,' Harrison said, pulling me out of my memories. 'I don't want to force you into anything, but just know that I'll do whatever my father tells me to do.'

'That spineless, are you?'

'Call it spineless all you want, but I'd like to think of it as sensible. A way to ensure self-preservation. A way to *survive.*'

'What kind of fucked-up world has my dad found himself in?'

Because I could hear the underlying threat in Harrison's words. Could hear what he was too afraid to say aloud.

Harold Baker was not a man to be trifled with.

He was a man used to getting his own way and would stop at nothing to ensure he got it, even go so far as marrying off his own son to grow his reach.

Oh, Daddy. What are you thinking?

'Arianna,' Harrison said, his eyes narrowing on my stricken face. 'I can't tell you much right now because who knows who's listening to us, but I'd like to take you out to dinner this week. If that's okay with you?'

'Do I have a choice?'

'You will always have a choice with me.' His tone was sombre, but the truth of his words hit me in the gut. 'I'm not that much of a villain.'

'So, you'll admit you're the villain?' I teased, biting my lip, trying to flirt with him but seeing it fall flat when he winced.

'Life is filled with villains. In every story, there is a hero and a villain. It all depends on who's telling the story, doesn't it?'

'I suppose so.'

'So, yeah, Arianna. I suppose I am the villain in yours.'

I blinked.

I hadn't expected him to admit it, but also, I wasn't even sure he was right. The villain here shared his initials, sure, but I didn't believe he was one for more than a second.

Okay.

Maybe it took a minute.

THIRTY
ROCK

age 18, march

THE MOMENT ARIANNA and Harrison left the room, I didn't know what the fuck to do—or where to look.

My mother had remained silent the entire meal, not wanting to say something that would embarrass her husband in front of a potential work alliance.

'Thank you so much for inviting us to dinner, Tony,' Harold said, leaning back in his chair and folding his hands over his large stomach. The buttons on his shirt were straining, struggling to keep his guts in, and I couldn't help but be repulsed by the greasy man sitting before me.

Everything about him screamed wrong!

'It was good of you to invite us so soon after your return.' Harold rubbed his large, protruding stomach, leaning back on the chair as if both stuffed and ready to eat more if the occasion arose. 'Harrison has bugged me for weeks to arrange this.'

'I didn't realise he'd already met Arianna,' Tony replied, a casual tone I'd heard him use over the years that hid his anger beneath it. He was extremely skilled at lulling people into a false sense of security—myself included at times—and then dropping the hammer on them when they were too deep and were unable to slither away without harm. 'You never mentioned that in any of our negotiations.'

I sat there, silent, my eyes travelling between them, not wanting to miss any word or expression from either of them. If I spoke, I might ruin the spell, and the two of them would clam up without revealing anything they shouldn't. Without a doubt, they were both decent poker players, able to twist their features to hide their true hand. The fact Arianna had become a *negotiation* sickened me. How dare they discuss and barter over her "hand in marriage" like we were living in the fucking 1800s? Bridgerton this was not.

'Ah,' Harold groaned, leaning forward once more. 'The little prick didn't tell me until a week ago, after he'd pestered me one too many times and I made sure to get to the bottom of it.'

What in the world is happening? My thoughts couldn't keep up with the very real, very bizarre situation we'd found ourselves in. Arranged marriages were outdated and Tony had never crossed me as the type to do something like that to his only daughter. But then again, the business meant everything to him. It was one of the reasons I was learning Business Studies at A-Level, after all. Tony made it clear it was the path he wanted for me, and after everything the guy had done for me over the last few years, I felt a debt to him I couldn't explain. He owned properties, which was his main focus, but there were other areas he dipped his toes in— he just wouldn't tell me about them until I graduated university.

It had never bothered me before, not knowing, but this dinner was making me doubt everything I thought I knew about Hollowdale Holdings.

'If they've already met, then our job should be easier,' Tony said with a deep chuckle. 'My Ari can be quite strong-willed when she wants.'

'And my Harrison will know exactly how to handle her, I can assure you.'

Nausea rose in my stomach at the way they were conversing

like me and mum weren't even there. Like Arianna wasn't a person with feelings and her own choice. They made her sound like an animal that needed to be tamed by a whip.

'Rock,' Tony called, bringing me into the fold once more. 'You know Arianna better than most.'

'Yes, sir.' My tone was clipped as I restrained myself from losing my temper with him.

'Are there any suitors we should be worried about? Any boys who could hinder our plan?'

I coughed, uncomfortable, because the answer was *me*. I was the *boy* ready to hinder their plan. I was the *suitor* they should worry about. But I couldn't say any of that, so I said what I could.

'Nobody I know of, sir. Arianna doesn't act like that.'

And somehow, even by trying to say the right thing, I managed to fuck it up and basically imply she was an untouched virgin. *Nice one, idiot.*

'I'm glad to hear she isn't like the loose girls these days,' Harold said, his eyes alight with amusement. 'Maybe our deal is worth more than originally thought.'

'We can always renegotiate terms,' Tony replied, smiling warmly at me, glad I helped him even if unwittingly. 'We have time.'

'But not too much time,' Harold warned. A chill ran through me at the serious expression he gave Tony and I wondered once more about just exactly what Tony had got himself into—and whether we should fear for our lives.

Or worse.

ARI AND HARRISON re-entered the dining room in silence, taking their positions at the table without comment about anything they'd just discussed.

The rest of the meal continued as if no major announcement had taken place. As if the parents hadn't disclosed more while they were gone, somehow thinking that I wouldn't give a shit about Arianna's hand being given away like she was a piece of property.

As soon as the Bakers left the house, I stalked Arianna up the stairs, wanting to catch her before she went into her bedroom. I knew she wanted to be alone, but I needed to talk to her first, and it couldn't wait.

'Wait up!' I hollered, and she paused, her hand on the doorknob, seconds away from disappearing inside to a place where I wouldn't just barge in on her. Back when we first became stepsiblings, we made it clear that our bedrooms were off-limits without an invitation. We had to knock and get a verbal response before entering. It was something I'd always honoured—except for that one time I burst in and found her half-dressed and stumbled out before I embarrassed us both, but now that we were a couple, I wasn't sure if the rules still applied, but I didn't want to push her over the edge so early on.

'Can we not talk about this here in the hall?'

'Are you inviting me in?'

'Just get in here, you big oaf.' She opened her door and I went on silent feet behind her, not wanting to spook her even though she knew I was following. Until I knew what she and Harrison had spoken about, I didn't want to just assume shit.

'What's going on?' I asked once the door was closed behind us and our parents wouldn't be able to overhear. 'Did you know anything about this?'

'What?' Ari turned menacing eyes to mine, livid. 'You think I knew about any of it and just, what, didn't give you a heads-up? Do you think so little of me?'

'Babe, you know that's not what I mean.'

'Do I? Because it sounds to me like you're accusing me of knowing I was *fucking engaged* and just didn't mention it to you when you asked me to be your girlfriend.'

Okay, so when she puts it like that, it doesn't sound so great.

'I'm sorry, Ari.' I reached out and pulled her closer, her small wrists in my hands delicate and dainty. 'I'm acting like an arse when you're the one who should be freaking. What did the two of you talk about?'

'He knew who I was at Gray's birthday party,' she said, her tone flat. 'Knew our fathers' had a plan, too. Just supposedly not exactly *what* the plan was. Not sure if I believe him or not.'

'That sucks.'

'That's a fucking understatement,' she spat, almost vibrating beneath my touch. 'It's manipulation at its finest.'

'That too.' I took a deep breath, encouraging her to do the same. 'What are you going to do about it?'

'Well, I'm not gonna marry him, that's for certain, but I need to find a way to break it off without ruining my dad's business shit.'

'Do you care enough? Your dad's trying to marry you off to someone for a *business deal* and you still want to do all you can to make him happy?'

'He's my dad.' She deflated in my arms, the full force of the evening's events hitting her in one fell swoop.

'Just because he's your dad, it doesn't mean he's not a complete cunt.'

She winced at my harsh words but didn't correct me. I'd never thought anything so harsh about Tony before, and it felt wrong to feel so strongly about the man who'd saved me and my mum from poverty.

'We won't let any of them get away with this shit, and you definitely aren't marrying that smooth-talking prick.'

'He *is* a smooth talker,' she said with the smallest hint of a smile. 'Why else would I spend the night with him?'

'Trying to make me jealous, babe?' I didn't add that it was totally fucking working.

'You had a girlfriend for *ages*, mister, so you've got no room to talk.'

'You also kissed Tyler multiple times over the last few years to make me jealous, so neither of us is a saint.'

I saw the moment my words sank in, and she gave a small nod in agreement, the most she'd do to acknowledge I had a fair point.

Since our heart-to-heart the other night, I felt like I knew Arianna even better. Knew why she'd made certain decisions—especially ones that involved Tyler—but a small pang of jealousy still travelled through me whenever I thought about it all.

'Neither of us is a saint,' she agreed. 'But I'm still the better person by far.'

'Keep telling yourself that, babe.' My hands went further south and I grabbed her bum, pulling her closer to me.

'I need to go out,' she blurted, moving herself out of my grasp and putting some distance between us. 'I'll be home later, okay?'

'You need to go out now? Right this moment?'

'Yeah,' she said, a vigorous nod accompanying it. 'It can't wait.'

'Okay…' I took a step away and let her move around her room, grabbing her bag and throwing some bits inside. We may be a couple, but I wasn't going to become an overbearing dickhead and demand she stay home. That wasn't going to win me any points in her eyes. 'Come to my room when you get home?'

She stopped and looked at me, an expression on her face I wasn't sure how to interpret.

'I'll text you,' was all she said.

Why was I getting the impression that my newfound relationship was about to go to shit before it had even had the chance to begin?

Ah, fuck.

Thirty-One

Arianna

age 18, march

I WAS SITTING cross-legged across from Gray, with him looking the epitome of casual, leaning up against his headboard, his legs stretched out in front of him.

When I left my house, I wasn't sure where to turn. I just knew I needed to get away.

At first, my feet started heading in the direction of the town centre, to where Tyler's flat was, but then I remembered how pissed Rock got at me for getting close to Tyler to make him jealous. Plus, I wasn't sure I could look into Tyler's eyes and admit the shit-heap my life had become overnight. Was it really only three nights ago I opened up to him? Wow, time moved fast.

So, my feet had taken me to Gray's instead, and even as I was on my way, I wondered with each breath whether I was making the right choice.

Maybe it would've been better to stay home and talk shit out with Rock—but he was who I needed to talk *about*, not talk *to*.

Ever since I'd got here, the two of us were making small talk, even though it was obvious we both needed to get our shit out in the open. After all, it felt weird to not be fully honest with Grayson. The two of us didn't do that with one another. It wasn't who we were.

Shit. Time to just get it out there. Blurt it out and rip that Band-Aid off.

Here goes nothing.

'I had sex with Rock,' I whispered, opening up to Gray the way I should've the last time I spoke to him and denied having any feelings for Rock whatsoever.

'No need to be ashamed about that, Ree. He split up with Savannah, didn't he?'

I nodded but didn't say anything. Gray quirked an eyebrow at me, confused at my reluctance to be happy about it.

'Did it only happen once?'

'Er…' I supposed it was only time to get it all out in the open. 'Not quite.'

'When?'

'The most recent time, or…?' I was evading and he could tell.

'I suppose all of it?'

'Okay.' I nodded and steeled my features. 'Last night.'

'And before that?'

'Beurrefest,' I whispered, shame spreading through me from head to toe. It was the worst thing I'd ever done, and I felt like such a trash human whenever I thought about it. Not because I was ashamed about having sex with Rock, but because he'd cheated on his girlfriend.

'I know about that, remember? You lost your virginity and then told him to jog on.'

I took a deep breath. 'No, the one just gone.'

'Fucking hell,' he said, shaking his head, a small smile on his face. 'Not beating around the bush, are you, Ree?'

'I was meant to tell you earlier, but I was scared.'

'Scared?' His eyes locked on mine and I saw the slight flicker of hurt that ran through them. 'Why would you be scared to tell me?'

'In case you judged me.'

'Why would I judge you for that? Fuck, Ree, I've been telling you for years to tell Rock how you feel. To take the bull by the horns and stop being afraid of everything.'

'There's something else, too,' I whispered, still not having come to terms with everything that had happened before I showed up at his door. 'I'm engaged.'

'Engaged?' he exclaimed, his eyes wider than I'd ever seen them. 'To *Rock*?'

'Nope. To that dude from your birthday party.'

'Who?'

'Exactly.' I bobbed my head, unable to believe it either. 'His name's Harrison, and our dads have decided we're going to marry for some business deal. Everything's just so fucked up.'

'I know,' he whispered, rubbing his jaw with his finger. 'Talking about things that are fucked up...'

'Go on,' I urged.

'I've got something to tell you.'

His words rang through the room, echoing off the walls and the ceiling, and it was the first time during the conversation that I looked at him.

Really looked at him.

He was tired. The circles under his eyes were darker than I'd seen them in some time. Although it was hard to see them through the bruises his brute of a dad left on him. Whenever Gray had a black eye, like he did at that moment, my heart bled for him more. He was my best friend. The best person I knew— besides Rock—and there was nothing I could do to help him. Nothing I could do to save him from the shitty existence he went home to every single night.

'You finally gonna tell me why you've been acting strange the last couple weeks?' I asked, leaning forward to watch his reaction. 'Or is it about that shiner you've been sporting since last weekend?'

'Bit of both, I guess.' He shrugged, looking away from my searing gaze, uncomfortable with my attention. Gray never liked to appear weak.

'Then hit me,' I said, getting comfortable and acting as if he wasn't about to say anything important. As if I didn't expect him to blow my world apart with his next sentence. Because I did expect him to do that. Things were strange between us, and the boy was keeping secrets from me. Something we promised never to do again after the summer there were rumours about me and a teacher from school hooking up and he didn't tell me about them until it was nearly too late. 'Least I can do, seeing as you've just listened to my crap.'

He nodded, preparing himself. A deep breath in. Out.

'Okay, so remember my birthday party?'

'Yes…' I said, dragging out the S. Of course I remembered his birthday party. It was the night everything happened—or so it seemed.

'You saw me go upstairs with Beth, right?'

I nodded. A small lie, but one I doubted he'd verify. I'd heard it from enough people to know it took place while I was outside with Harrison.

'We fucked that night.'

'*Shit*,' I spat out, my eyes widening on his face. My eyes were also widening at the blunt way he'd said the words, like he didn't even know it until recently. Like he was *telling* me something I didn't know. *Stupid boy*. I couldn't help myself from asking, 'Have you only just realised?'

'Sort of…' he trailed off and I wanted to hit him across the head, but I refrained. 'I still can't really remember much of that night.'

'You were plastered,' I said, unable to stop acting like his older sister for even a moment. 'I warned you not to get so drunk so fast!'

'Yes, Mum, I remember. But either way, I don't remember it, and I feel like fucking shit about it because she was a virgin.'

'Fucking hell, Grayson. And you've just been dating the girl, not even knowing you've already had sex with her?'

The boy visibly winced and I knew I'd hit a nerve. Gray was

already feeling crappy about it—trust me to make him feel worse.

'I suppose,' he said with a shrug, his face crumbling. 'But that's not even the worst of it.'

'I mean, can it get much worse?' A small laugh left my lips unbidden, but the seriousness of the expression Gray gave me put a stop to it real fast.

'Yeah, Ree. It can.'

I raised an eyebrow and stayed silent, waiting for him to continue. Gray sat forward, no longer relaxed enough to lounge back, and I took a deep breath for whatever came next.

'Beth's pregnant.'

'She's what now?' My voice was so loud, I covered my mouth with my hand, surprised at myself. Surprised by my reaction.

'Beth's pregnant,' he repeated, his tone sombre. When I looked at him—really looked at him—I could tell it was eating him up inside. That I was only seeing the surface of his emotions.

'She told you that?' I asked, not wanting to sound like I didn't believe her, but also wanting to establish that it wasn't something Gray had thought he heard or some crap.

'Yep.' His eyes met mine, staring at me before he blinked and averted his gaze. 'Last weekend.'

'Shit.' My mind went back to the previous weekend, and an image of Gray's beaten face entered it. 'She didn't give you the black eye, did she?'

'She's not a bitch, Ree,' he said with a deep sigh that made me feel only *slightly* guilty for having thought that about Beth. 'But no, that's courtesy of the old man.'

'Oh.'

'Yeah. Oh.'

'What are you gonna do about it? Is she going to have an abortion?'

Gray's face went pale, a stricken expression covering his face, and I guessed he hadn't considered that as a possibility. Of course he hadn't. Gray accepted his lot in life, no matter how bad things were, and he never thought of himself getting out of a situation. He learned of Beth's pregnancy and accepted it, even if he didn't like it.

'I don't know,' he croaked. 'It didn't even enter my mind.'

'That she may want that?'

'That it was even a thing she could do. All I've been thinking about the last week is a way we can make it work. A way the two of us can bring a life into the world. *This* world. And have it be a normal, healthy, and okay situation.'

'Any solutions?' I wasn't overly hopeful, but I asked anyway. Maybe Gray had thought of something in the last week that wasn't obvious straight away.

'Not one.'

His admission cut me deep. The look on his face, the effort in those two words, killed me inside. My best friend was struggling and all I'd cared about was my relationship with my stepbrother. I was a shit friend.

'Have you not spoken about it?'

'I—' he paused, sitting up even straighter, and looked me dead in the eye. 'I haven't spoken to her at all.'

'*At all?*'

'No...' He glanced away, avoiding my eyes the way he'd avoided Beth.

My glare was an accusation. I couldn't say I was a huge Beth Jacobs fan or anything, but she didn't deserve the way Gray was treating her.

Nobody did.

'I've avoided her,' he whispered.

'Jesus, Gray! I didn't think you were that much of a dickhead. If I didn't want to hug you, I'd smother you.'

'I'll take the hug.' He leaned forward, and I put my arms around him, pulling him close to my chest. He mumbled into my jumper, 'I'm sorry. I fucked up.'

'Don't be apologising to me. I only learned about it five minutes ago. The person you should be apologising to is your girl.' I took a deep breath, not wanting to sound like I was admonishing him too hard, but also at the same time, I wanted to make it clear how disappointed I was in his actions. *He really can be such a dumb boy.* 'You've really let her down. I can't even imagine the worries going through her mind right now. The fear. The absolute shame and terror of the kids at school learning about it.'

'You can't tell anybody.' He broke free from my hug, his eyes wide and scared. As if he thought that of me. As if I was the kind of person to go around and spread harmful gossip for the sake of it.

'Who do you think I am? Of course I'm not gonna tell anybody.'

I shuffled closer to Gray so he could hug me. I knew he needed it. His nose buried in my hair, and he inhaled dramatically.

'Dude. Are you smelling my head?'

'Just let me have this.'

'Gray,' I whispered, my words muffled from where I was pulled up against Gray's chest. 'You have to talk to her. Listen to her. Let her cry. Comfort her. Whatever she needs, you have to do it. Fuck, man, you've got to grovel on your fucking knees and apologise until you're blue in the face.'

The two of us fell silent, both deep in thought, wondering just exactly what the future held.

THIRTY-TWO
ROCK

age 18, march

ARIANNA HAD LEFT. Had gone out of the house and left me alone and for what reason? To meet with Grayson.

To go spend time with her best friend, rather than spending time with me, her boyfriend, when things were already so uncertain between us.

Did it hurt? Fuck yeah, it did. My girl wanted to spend time with Grayson, and there was fuck all I could do about it.

She'd always been close with him, and the two of them had always had a close bond that others couldn't compete with, but I suppose I never thought it was me who would be competing with it.

She'd left hours ago, and ever since she'd gone, I'd stayed in my room, lying on my bed and watching the ceiling, letting my thoughts run awry.

Arianna was everything I'd always wanted—something I never thought possible, but what I'd held out hope for all those years while we played pretend nonetheless. Yet the reality wasn't matching up and I wasn't sure how to handle that. I knew it was stupid to have put it—put *her*—on a pedestal in my mind, like something unattainable, but I'd done it anyway, never believing I'd experience anything other than admiring her from afar.

I waited for her text to tell me she was on her way home.

I waited for her to at least let me know where she was and not to worry about her.

So far, she'd done neither.

So, I lay in my bed and dreamed of our future. A future I wanted more than anything. One I still wasn't sure how to achieve, what with our parents and Ari's *engagement* being an obstacle and all that, but one I believed we would obtain because we were determined and we loved each other.

I waited so long I fell asleep, the thoughts of Arianna playing on my mind, and it wasn't until a knock came on my bedroom door that I awoke. I wondered why she hadn't thought to use the jack-and-jill bathroom that connected our rooms instead now our parents were home again, but maybe she'd not remembered in her rush to see me. The thought made my heart swell, just a little.

'Come in,' I called out, my words sleep filled. My eyelids peeled open, the light from the crack in the door harsh, to find Ari standing there, looking sheepish.

'Sorry,' she whispered. 'I can come back later.'

'When our parents are awake?' I laughed, staying quiet so I didn't wake said parents. Not really a way to explain Ari sneaking into my bedroom in the early hours of the morning. 'Get in here before someone sees you.'

She tiptoed inside, closing the door with a gentle push, and came over to my bed. She was wearing the same clothes she left the house in and I knew she'd come straight up to my room without visiting her own first.

'I'm sorry I didn't text you.'

'That's okay,' I replied half-heartedly. 'I fell asleep so wouldn't have read it anyway.'

'I thought maybe you'd have gone to see the guys.' She sat on the edge of my bed, but I reached out to pull her down beside me, lifting the cover so she could join me beneath it. 'Didn't think you'd stay home.'

'Why wouldn't I?' I shuffled to my side to face her and she did the same. 'I don't feel the need to escape all the time.'

'Ouch.' She rubbed her hand over her heart, her eyes downcast. 'Wounding me deep, babe.'

'It's true.' Our voices were hushed, barely a whisper, but our faces were so close together it still felt loud in the empty room. 'You always run off to Grayson or Tyler when things get tough.'

'That's not fair.'

'Isn't it?' Hurt seeped in. 'Because that's how it looks to me.'

'I—'

'No, let me get this out while it's dark.'

'Okay,' she hushed out.

'It kills me you run off to Gray and feel like you can't talk to me. We're meant to be a team, babe, but when you talk to everyone else, how can we be?'

'It was one night,' she replied. 'But also, how am I meant to talk about you to you?'

'You shouldn't want to talk about me.'

'I'm not saying I want to talk bad things about you.' She shook her head. 'I just needed an outsider's perspective.'

'And Grayson's that person?'

'Would you prefer it to be Tyler?' she snapped, and my heart sank.

'That's a low blow, babe,' I replied, sad but not surprised she'd instantly gone for the jugular. She had a habit of doing that when she felt trapped.

'I'm sorry.' A tear travelled down her cheek. 'I'm sorry I'm such a bitch to you. I don't mean to be.'

'I know, but sometimes actions speak just as loud as words, Ari, and you're not always great at either.'

'Are you trying to rub it in?'

'No.' My heart physically hurt thinking I'd upset her, but there were so many times when she'd upset me and I'd given her a free pass because of my feelings for her that I couldn't let it slide anymore. Not if the two of us were going to work through all obstacles and still come out standing strong. 'I want you to know how I feel, though.'

The tears were falling in earnest, and I wanted to wipe away each one and kiss it better, but it was because of me they were there, so it didn't feel right to.

'Talking with you is hard,' she said with a swallow. 'I can talk to Gray and Ty because I never worry what they'll think of me—not really. With you, I never want you to think poorly of me, so it's easier not to tell you things. We've spent so many years keeping our distance, and even when we didn't, all we'd do was fight the sexual tension creeping between us, that I don't know how to make things right.'

'We're together now.'

'Yes.'

'That's all that matters. As long as we're together, we can overcome all the shit thrown our way, but in order for that to happen, you need to talk to me and not run away from our problems. Okay?'

'Okay,' she whispered, and I knew I had to tell her how I felt. The true depth of my feelings for her, not just some vague sentiment about liking her or finding her attractive, but the real deal.

'I love you.' I kept my eyes on her, not wanting to look away, but also in fear, looking for a flicker on her face to let me know she didn't reciprocate.

'I love you, too.' Her eyes wrinkled at the edges, and all I could do was breathe a huge sigh of relief.

Thank fuck for that.

Thirty-Three

Arianna

age 18, march

'Are you sure you can't get out of it?' I'd whined a mere hour ago, not wanting to sound like a spoiled brat, but knowing that was exactly how I sounded.

'Mum really wants me to come out to dinner with her, babe. I've not spent time with her in ages and it's the least I can do.' Rock kissed my forehead, a soft graze of his lips, and I instantly warmed at his touch. He was my rock, and whenever he was around, I was rooted. 'Your dad's away, so there's no need to worry he'll ambush you. You'll be fine here.'

That was what Rock had told me moments before he left, but ten minutes after he and Gigi had gone, a knock came at the front door.

Harrison was standing on the other side, looking as charming as the night we met, but with a sinister smirk playing on his lips.

Ever since my dad had thrown the whole engagement thing in my face, I'd managed to push off any plans to put me and Harrison in the same room together. I'd made plans anytime he asked me to dinner, or on a date, and when Dad invited Harold and Harrison over to dinner, I was noticeably absent. But not tonight.

My dad had somehow cornered me, even while out of the

country, and I hadn't even realised it until it was too late. Must be why Gigi was so adamant Rock went out with her to dinner.

'Evening,' Harrison greeted me, reaching out his hand for me to shake. 'Thanks for inviting me.'

'I—'

'I was starting to think you were avoiding me,' he continued, as if I hadn't tried to speak at all.

'I—'

'These are for you.' He handed me a large bouquet of flowers and I took them, still unable to speak, so blindsided by his appearance. Stupid me had thought I was free from my dad's machinations while he was away, but I'd underestimated his determination to make this engagement stick. *Stupid Ari.*

'Thanks,' I stammered, my heart rate spiking. 'I'm sorry I'm not dressed for…' I trailed off, unsure what he'd been told our plans were. Maybe he was here to take me out of the house, and that just wasn't going to fly with me.

Never let them take you to a second location.

'Didn't you invite me here for dinner?'

'Er…' I looked around, hoping a member of staff would appear and save me, but there was nobody around. 'Let me go check with the kitchen if there's something for us to have.'

He nodded, still standing on the other side of the doorstep, an understanding smile having replaced the sinister smirk. 'Is it okay for me to come in?'

Not really, I wanted to say, but instead, I nodded and opened the door wider so he could enter without grazing against me. My dad was sneaky, and if I wasn't so mad at him, I'd probably admire his tenacity. It was where I'd got it from, after all. My dad's skill at never taking no for an answer in business had always impressed me, until he'd turned it on me and put me in the firing zone.

'Just stay here, okay?' I didn't wait to hear his answer and headed off in the direction of the staff kitchen hidden at the back of the house. Dad had wanted us to have a kitchen we could use if we wanted, but one staff could use when entertaining guests, so it made total sense to him to have two installed. 'Mr Billins,' I called out, hoping he'd pop his head out his office door as I passed, but he didn't. 'Mr Billins!'

He appeared in the hallway, like a spectre, and I near jumped out of my skin.

'Mr Billins, you scared me,' I said, as if the jump I'd made three feet in the air hadn't given it away. To his credit, his smile never changed as he let me compose myself. 'Harrison Baker has arrived for dinner?'

I wasn't meant to ask it as a question.

'Yes, miss,' he replied, waiting for me to continue.

'Were we...' I struggled to find the right word, looking around me for inspiration, then getting pissed at myself when nothing came. 'Expecting him?'

'We were, miss. Your father left instructions before he went away.'

'Oh.'

'Would you like time to change, miss?'

'I—' I thought about it for a brief moment. Changing would at least give me time to collect myself and think of a game plan. Plus, Harrison couldn't follow me upstairs with the staff watching. 'Yes, please.'

'And shall I take Mister Baker through to the dining room to wait for you there? And put those flowers in a vase for you?'

I'd forgotten I was still holding on to the flowers with a vice-like grip.

'Please,' I said, handing over the flowers, thankful he was giving me a chance to breathe. Maybe he could tell from the terror on my face that I was blindsided by his arrival.

On quick feet, I made my way to my bedroom, closing the door behind me and locking it once inside, not leaving anything to chance.

I dressed, my thoughts running a mile a minute, and even after having taken twenty minutes to make myself more presentable, I still wasn't any closer to having a game plan in place.

My dad had outsmarted me and I had no idea how to outsmart him back.

When we'd spoken last, Harrison hadn't seemed opposed to the arranged marriage. If anything, he'd seemed an eager and willing participant, which meant I wasn't going to find a conspirator in him, either.

Surely this isn't real life?

I read books and often watched films where things like arranged marriages and forced engagements happened, but never had I believed they happened in real life. Not in this day and age.

But I was wrong, just the same as I was wrong about so much in life. It was getting a bit boring how little I really knew.

After half an hour of pottering around in my bedroom, pretending I was getting ready, I knew I couldn't put it off any longer. Slowly, with silent footsteps, I crept down the stairs and walked to the formal dining room. When I entered, I found Harrison pacing the small space beside the table, his gaze on his feet but tracking up to mine when he spotted me.

'You look beautiful,' he hushed, his eyes wide and impressed. 'I apologise if I was earlier than you expected.'

'I lost track of time,' I said, not wanting to admit I hadn't known he was coming. I couldn't suss him out enough to know whether giving him the truth was a good idea or not. That night at Grayson's party, I thought I'd got a measure of him, but when he'd shown up for that disastrous dinner and told me he'd known who I was all along, I'd realised I didn't know him at all. 'Thank you for coming.'

'The pleasure really is all mine, Arianna.'

'Please,' I said, moving around the table on the other side to where he was standing, and took my seat. 'Call me Ari.'

'Ari,' he murmured, taking his seat after me. The flowers he'd handed me, that I'd passed to Mr Billins, were sitting in a vase in the centre next to a lit candelabra. 'Thank you for inviting me.'

I didn't have the heart to admit I hadn't. So, I stayed quiet.

Why was silence so horrible with some people and so blissful with others? With Rock, silence was anything but uncomfortable. It was peace and love, all things good in my life.

The silence between me and Harrison was anything but that. It was awkward, strained, and everything wrong in my life.

'So…' he started once our glasses were filled and our starters placed in front of us. 'Have you had time to think about what I said?'

'What part?' Was it bad I couldn't remember much of what he'd said to me at the dinner? I was so blindsided and ready to get out of the room and tell Rock everything that I'd forgotten most of it. Or maybe I'd pushed it to the back of my mind because I didn't want to live in reality. Dissociation at its finest.

Either way, my mind was drawing a blank.

'The part about going on dates and getting to know each other better.'

'Oh, that part. I—'

'Before you say anything,' he interrupted, placing his elbows on the table and resting his hands under his chin to lean closer to me, 'I want you to know that I know about you and Rock.'

'Huh?'

'I could see the looks passing between you at dinner. You weren't exactly inconspicuous or anything.' He laughed, and I gave a nervous laugh in return, feeling myself sink deeper into despair. 'And it was clear to me your dad is blind to the situation. Tell me. How long have you two been hiding under their noses?'

I didn't respond, not wanting to confirm his suspicions and fan the flames without him having concrete evidence. There was no way to know whether he'd pass it along to our fathers the moment he left the dining room.

'It's a recent development at least,' he continued, as if he hadn't just asked me a question that I'd refused to answer. 'Because back in February, you were single.'

'What makes you so sure of that?'

'Ari, you're not the type of girl to cheat on somebody.'

Nope. Just the kind who will sleep with somebody else's boyfriend.

I hated that he had me pegged so thoroughly and in such a short amount of time, too.

'And Rock was nowhere to be seen when I stole you away from the party,' he continued, as if the terror playing out on my face wasn't a concern of his. 'The way he acted at dinner… well, there's no way he wouldn't have found us that night if you two were a couple.'

'Hmm,' I hummed, taking a sip of my wine. *Just stay silent, Ari. Don't give him an inch.*

'There's no need to be so shy with me,' he said, a small laugh leaving his lips. 'We're to be married, after all.'

'You seem very sure about that,' I replied, unable to bite my tongue.

'And you're not?'

'A lot can happen in a short space of time,' I said, thinking back on the last few months and how fast everything had changed.

'It can indeed,' he agreed. 'Which is why I'm not fazed in the slightest about this news. At the end of the day, Ari, you'll be my wife. Not his. And then what will you two do about it?'

'You seem awfully sure you know the truth about Rock and me.'

'You don't hide it.'

'We don't flaunt it, either,' I snapped.

He seemed to take that as an admission of guilt. *Silly me.*

'And you will never flaunt it,' he said, leaning back in his chair, all the while keeping his intense gaze on me. 'Because once you're my wife, you will never be alone with him again.'

'He's my stepbrother.'

His tone darkened. 'He's a problem.'

DINNER WAS STILTED and I wanted nothing more than to get out of there, but there was no way to do so. Once the dessert plates were taken away, we retreated into the living room, and I'd hoped the change of scenery would make things feel less awkward. It was wishful thinking.

'You stayed so quiet throughout dinner,' Harrison said, moving to sit on one of the sofas. 'Even now you're still sitting in silence. Are you feeling okay?'

'Of course I'm not feeling okay,' I hissed. 'I'm being forced into something I don't want and you don't seem to give a fuck.'

'It's not that I don't give a fuck.'

'What is it then?'

'It's that I know when to rebel and when to do as I'm told.' He brushed his hand through his hair in agitation. 'And this is one of the situations where it's best to do as I'm told, at least to begin with. Maybe in a month or two, our dads will calm down or realise we don't need to marry for their business shit to work out.'

'Why do we even *need* to marry in the first place?' I asked, frustrated, but not at him. 'Not like I've got anything business wise your dad would want.'

'You're Tony Hollowdale's only heir, right?'

'Technically,' I agreed. 'But Rock's the one he's been training up. The one taking business at school and heading off to university and whatever. I'm just his daughter.'

'A daughter is a great bargaining tool.'

'So I've discovered,' I said, my tone dry. 'I've been reduced to a pawn on a chessboard as opposed to a real human being.'

Harrison stood from his lounged position and came to sit beside me, his arm reaching out to lounge across my shoulder, but I darted away fast enough that it flopped to his side instead.

It meant I was basically sitting on the arm of the sofa, but it was worth it to put distance between us.

'I see you as a real human being.'

'Really?' *Why do I find that so hard to believe?*

'Really,' he said with a firm nod of his head. 'I never want to make you feel otherwise.'

'Could've fooled me,' I muttered.

'I've been respectful, haven't I?' The words were nice, but the tone made something inside me squirm. Why would a respectful person feel the need to point out they'd acted respectfully if it was something they did in general?

A chill ran down my spine. Was the room getting colder, or was it me?

'Yes...'

'I've let you carry out your rebellion against your dad and not said shit against it.'

I sputtered. 'Rebellion?'

'Yet you still aren't giving me a proper chance.'

'I'm sorry but—'

'You're not sorry,' Harrison spat, slowly working himself up, his face growing redder with every second. 'You're just another one of those stuck-up brats who think they can get everything they want.'

'Wait a moment!'

'You sit there, looking a million pounds, like you've made a real effort for me, yet you still have the cheek to reject me. Me!'

His hand darted from where he'd placed it on the sofa onto my leg, gripping me and keeping me in place so I couldn't get away. His hand was hot, leaving an imprint on me, and even shuffling as far away as I could, there wasn't anywhere for me to go unless I decided to commit to falling to the floor, which I was certain wouldn't help.

'Going somewhere?' he grumbled, gripping me tighter.

'I think I should go see if somebody can get us some drink

refills,' I said, trying my best to stand and get away from his grip on my thigh.

'I think we've both had enough to drink.'

'Are you sure?' I asked, keeping my tone breezy and unaffected. 'I'm sure there's a fifty-year-old whiskey somewhere.'

'Why, Arianna, you're a bit of a bore, aren't you? Would you rather go off in search of a drink than sit here in my company?'

'No,' I bit out through gritted teeth, even though that was exactly what I wanted. 'I just didn't want you to think I was a bad hostess.'

'Why don't you sit a little closer?' he asked, his voice dripping poison. 'If we're to marry, it only makes sense to see if we're compatible.'

'I'm okay where I am, thank you.'

'Shame.' The one word travelled through me and sent a chill right down to my bones. It was insincere, like the rest of him was turning out to be, and I knew he didn't give a shit about me.

He was playing an act, most likely since the night I met him, and I was a fool for believing if I spoke to him alone, he'd call off the engagement.

'Oh, gee,' I said, mustering a brightness I didn't feel. 'Look at the time!' I made a big deal of checking my watch and turning to look into his eyes. 'I think it's best you head off now. Wouldn't want to keep you from whatever fun plans you've got tonight.'

'You're my only plan, Arianna.'

I was afraid of that.

'I plan to turn in soon,' I said, wondering if anybody would believe I wanted to go to bed at just gone ten on a Friday night. 'I've had a stressful week.'

'Let me help to de-stress you,' Harrison said, his grip loosening on my leg, but if I was hoping he'd take it away completely, then I clearly didn't see the situation for what it was. His hand began to caress my thigh, slowly, languishing up and down in a soft, gentle movement. One I most definitely didn't want, but being trapped between him and the arm of the sofa meant I had little choice. 'It can't be easy, having to pretend all the time.'

'I don't have to pretend all the time.'

'Hm,' he mused, studying my face. 'Even now you feel you have to pretend with me.' His other hand came up to touch my face, down my nose, along my cheekbone, and into my hair.

A noise came from the hall, followed by hurried footsteps, and I seized an opportunity. 'Is that Mr Billins? Maybe you can call out to him now for some more wine.'

'But I didn't want any.'

'But I did,' I pointed out. I didn't, but at least with Harrison focused on the door and the potential chance of getting Mr Billins's attention to get *my* attention, I was able to slip out of the gap on the sofa and stand, freeing myself from his ministrations. 'No wine for me, actually, I really must depart for bed.'

Harrison's eye flickered, and his eyebrow twitched, rising when he noticed me standing, edging closer to the door step by step. 'Going somewhere, darling?'

'Yes,' I replied firmly. 'To bed, which means you must leave.'

'It means nothing of the sort.'

'You're not joining me if that's what you're implying,' I snapped. 'I bid you good night, Harrison Baker.'

'Arianna Hollowdale,' he said, his teeth on show. Sinister and sharpened. Ready for the kill. 'You take one step closer to the door and I swear I'll tell everybody about you and Rock. I'll tell your dad and mine, who won't be very happy when they hear their deal is on the verge of falling through. Men like that are never pleased to have a woman fuck up their plans. I can assure you of that.'

'Are you threatening me?' The breath left my throat as I wondered when I'd lost such control over my own life.

'Why, yes. Yes, I am.' His smile widened, the oozing of smugness radiating from him in waves. 'And I shall continue to do so until you do as you're told.' He stood, matching my defiant stance, and cocked his head. 'You see, the thing is, I've been nice to you when others wouldn't have given you the time of day. I've treated you like a human and not property, have I not?'

I remained silent, watching the truth reveal itself in front of me. Harrison was attractive and well-off, but he was also cruel and on the verge of villainy.

His words from our conversation after the engagement announcement came back to me, like a ghostly whisper in the wind.

'*Life is filled with villains. In every story, there is a hero and a villain… I suppose I am the villain in yours.*'

He'd told me the truth, and I'd been too blind to see it for what it was.

'One day very soon, Arianna,' he continued, his eyes narrowed on mine, 'you *will* be my property, and you won't have the choice you do now to refuse me.' He took a step closer, and I took a step back. Once more, I found myself in a dance of footsteps with a guy, but not one I wanted to partake in. 'So, you can either work with me and make this arrangement work for us, or you can defy me and see what it gets you.'

'I'm not *defying you*, as you so kindly put it,' I scoffed. 'I'm standing up for myself and for what I believe in. I never agreed to marry you, and I never even agreed to this fucking dinner! I think you should leave before Rock gets home.'

'You're engaged to *me* not him and it would do you best to remember that.'

'Or what? You going to force me, Harrison?'

I laughed, feeling not one ounce of the bravery I was projecting, and stood my ground—literally—when all I wanted to do was run out of the room and bolt myself somewhere he couldn't reach me.

The look in his eye and the cockiness of his words had me doubting I'd ever met the real Harrison. The Harrison of Grayson's party was a mirage, a pretender, a *lie*. He'd known who I was and the plan to have us marry, and had played me like putty. Even if he'd said he didn't. I felt it deep down in my gut.

'Force you?' he growled, still standing a short distance away. 'Why would I ever need to force you when you want me just as much as I want you?'

'You're fucking deluded.'

His left eye twitched again.

'And you're a fucking bitch.' He flew forwards and I didn't have time to move before he was grabbing me by the shoulders and throwing me into the wall. My back slammed against it and pain reverberated through me, the shock of it causing me to lose my breath, having had it knocked right out of me. 'You think you're so high and mighty, flaunting your beauty in my face and then denying me. Acting as if I'm the villain in your story.'

I was trying to catch my breath, but the panic was slowly taking over and causing my body to turn statue-still, and there was nothing I could do about it. Panic overwhelmed me.

One hand kept my shoulder pushed against the wall while the other began to travel down to grope my breast.

A whimper left my lips.

My legs turned to jelly and I was frozen in time, unable to breathe or move or do anything to save myself.

Fuck.

THIRTY-FOUR
ROCK

age 18, march

'WHAT THE FUCK is going on here?'

The door slammed open and hit the wooden panel with a cracking sound, but I didn't look around to see if it had. My focus was on the two people tangled together in front of me.

The look on Arianna's face told me enough.

'I'm going to fucking kill you!' I shouted, throwing myself on Harrison, wanting nothing more than to rip him off Ari and then rip his fucking head off. How dare he touch her when she didn't want him to?

What a sick prick.

'How dare you touch her, you fucking dickhead! Did you even ask before you put your hands all over her?'

'Rock!' Ari shouted, tears filling her red-rimmed eyes.

My fist collided with Harrison's face, and he stumbled back and away from her, his face one of shock.

But I didn't give it much thought as I followed his step back and used his surprise to my advantage by hitting him again, even harder than before.

All my pent-up rage at the situation—at him—bubbled up and out until I couldn't control it any longer.

My fists wouldn't stop.

216

My rage was endless.

Arianna was screaming; shouting. Harrison was silent, taking every blow I aimed his way.

And it was only when his blood covered my hands and his face was unrecognisable that I stopped.

That I came to and saw the damage I'd delivered.

But even then, I didn't care. He deserved every last blow, both to his body and to his ego, the little prick.

Nobody touched my girl without consequence.

Nobody.

HARRISON LEFT NOT long after he dragged himself up from the floor and walked away without a backward glance, leaving a trail of blood in his wake.

I didn't give a fuck, though. If anything, I wished I'd hurt him more than I did. The fact he *walked* out of the house was a sour point in my eyes. Putting his hands on my girl should mean he never walked again. Would never have the chance to do the same thing to some other innocent girl who rejected his advances.

Arianna had fled to her room not long after, refusing to answer my mum's questions, and I followed her, not wanting her to be left alone.

'Ari,' I said, standing on the threshold of her bedroom, not wanting to enter without her permission. 'Can I come in?'

She was a mass of covers on her bed, having completely covered herself the moment she landed on her bed, and I saw the duvet move in a small nod.

'Baby, talk to me.' I perched on the edge of her bed so I wouldn't crowd her, but also not wanting to be too far away either. Seeing her that way had made my heart break. I'd already figured out she was my forever, but seeing her like that, being held against her will, was enough for me to know I would never leave her side. She was it for me. The one I wanted to protect forevermore. No matter how whipped that made me sound. I was sure the guys would laugh at me, but I didn't care. Ari was more important than any of them and their opinions.

'I don't know what to say.' Her voice came muffled through the cover, but I could still make out her form—or assumed I could—so I went to rub her back, but thought better of doing it without letting her know first.

'Can I touch you?' I asked, softening my voice, as if talking to a child. Her nod came once more, and I began to run my hand up and down her back, slow and steady. 'You don't need to talk to me tonight. Fuck, if you don't want to talk to me about it at all, I'll completely understand and I won't push you. But, baby, please, talk to somebody when you're ready.'

Like a caterpillar emerging from its cocoon, no longer a caterpillar but a butterfly, Ari came out from underneath the cover, her red-rimmed eyes hurting me to the core. 'Thank you.'

'You never need to thank me,' I said, my voice wavering. 'We're a team, aren't we?'

Now that I knew she wasn't going to bolt, I moved back a little on the bed to rest my back up against the wall her bed was adjacent to. Ari sniffed, moving to lay her head on my lap, a small whisper barely heard. 'We're a team. Always.'

'And I'm not saying it needs to be soon,' I started, voicing the thoughts running through my mind, 'but I want everyone to know about us. Not just our friends, but *everybody*, including our parents.'

Her only response was a move of her head, brushing up against the zipper of my jeans. All it took was the events of the evening flashing through my mind's eyes for my dick to know it wasn't the time to get excited from the friction.

'No more fake engagements, no more pretending we don't

want each other or care for one another. All that bullshit is over. Our parents will have to like it or lump it. Simple as.'

'But what if they get mad?' Her voice was small and uncertain.

'Then they get mad.' I shrugged, not knowing what else to say. I was over making anyone but us happy. For years I'd stayed away from Ari so my mum could be happy, and look where that had gotten us all. 'But that isn't our problem. We're eighteen and therefore classed as legal adults. We've got every right to live our lives on our own terms, babe. And from today, that's what's going to happen.'

'You make it sound so simple.'

'Isn't it?'

'Well, if it's so fucking simple, then why have we stayed away from each other for so long?'

'Because you told me to get the fuck away from you,' I said with a small laugh. I was over it now, but at the time, it had hurt the way she'd pushed me away moments after we'd crossed that bridge together and shed our virginities. The way she always told me our timing was off.

'I—' She stopped herself from continuing, no doubt about to dig herself a hole she didn't have the current strength to climb out of and then thought better of it. 'I'm sorry.'

'What do you have to be sorry for, babe?'

'For waiting so long to confess how I truly felt about you and for how silly I acted all the times in between.'

'Then I should apologise too because you weren't alone in those things,' I said, feeling bad she thought she needed to apologise to me. We were both at fault. Yeah, for different reasons, but still at fault nonetheless.

'We're both silly twats then.' She laughed, and her hand came from underneath her head and grazed mine, the slight pressure of her fingertips sending shockwaves through me. Just the slightest touch, and she made me want more. 'Because neither of us spoke out when she should've.'

'True,' I said, gripping my fingers with hers. 'And I suppose that isn't the most important part of it all, anyway.'

'What is then?' she asked, her voice genuine, wanting to know my answer.

'The fact we came to our senses in the end, of course. That we're together now and ready to take on the world.'

'And by world you mean…' She sat up, looking at me for the first time since we came upstairs.

'I mean our parents. We need to talk to them and let the chips fall where they may.' It wasn't the first time I'd said it, but it was the first time I thought Ari would actually agree with me on the best course of action.

I waited for her to reply, not wanting to influence her either way.

'You're right,' she breathed out, a small smile playing on her plump lips. 'Your mum's home for who knows how long and Dad plans to join her, so we need to strike while the iron is scalding. I'll text Dad and request a family dinner for tomorrow night. The man can come back from wherever he is, can't he?'

'Tomorrow night?' I asked, surprised she was listing a date so soon. I thought she'd come around to my way of thinking, but still want a week or so to prepare what she was gonna say to them. 'Are you sure that isn't a little *too* soon?'

'No.' Her eyes turned to steel. 'He needs to know Harrison is gone, never to return. But he also needs to respect that he won't be setting me up with any of his other business friends' sons either. I'm not his pawn and I won't be used as such.'

'Only if you're sure.' I never wanted her to do something she wasn't ready for, especially after what had happened earlier that night. My heart still wasn't recovered so there was no way hers was, either.

'Rock, we'll never be able to move on with our lives if we don't do this.'

'You're right,' I told her, gazing into her jade eyes. 'Are you sure you're ready?'

'I'm ready to talk to our parents, but I'm not ready just yet to talk about what happened earlier.'

'I'll be here whenever you are.' And I meant it. I wasn't going to push, and I didn't want her to do anything she wasn't ready to do. 'But there's no rush.'

'Have I told you I love you?'

'Not today,' I said in an attempt to alleviate some of the tension that had crept into the room. 'And have I told you I love you, too?'

'You mighta mentioned it once or twice, but it's something I'll never get tired of hearing, so you may want to say it more.'

'If I say it with every sentence, it'll lose its importance.'

'Never.' Her one word whispered across my face, and I took it in, breathing in the simplicity of it.

Thirty-five

Arianna

age 18, march

THE NEXT NIGHT, I knew we needed to tell our parents the truth.

I also needed to tell my dad that under no circumstances would I marry Harrison Baker, and that he may want to come to terms with the fact he won't be going into business with Harold Baker either.

Neither thing was going to go down well.

'How do we even start the conversation?' I asked.

Rock looked at me, his face blank. The whole night—well, maybe not the whole night, but a large part of it—we'd discussed what to say to our parents, but not quite how to actually *start* the conversation.

'Huh?'

'How do we start? We sit down for dinner, we wait until the main course, and then say… what exactly?'

'Surely your dad must know the engagement's off,' Rock said, and I shook my head in reply.

'Why would he? He wasn't home last night and I highly doubt your mum told him any of it.'

'Mum's not a monster, Ari.' His face contorted and a stab of guilt went through me for insulting his mum. I hadn't meant to.

'No, she's not, but she lives a comfortable life, plus loves my dad, so she's not going to hinder that for me, is she? Not sure she even knows the true extent of what went down, anyway.'

'We sit down. We eat. Then we say: We have something we wanted to talk to you about, or something along those lines.'

'Right…' I looked around the room, thinking of all the things that could go wrong with that.

'You don't sound very sure,' Rock said, seeing right through me. 'What do you think's gonna happen?'

My stomach dropped, leaving me as I thought about what could happen. Would my dad hit Rock? Would he refuse to listen or cut me off?

I hated the unknown, and this was definitely something unknown.

'It'll be fine, babe,' Rock said, placing a chaste kiss on my head. 'We've got this. It's you and me. Who cares what they say or think?'

'If you say so…' I said, leaning into his warmth, wanting to steal some of his strength to take with me into dinner. 'Just remember to save me when I need it.'

'I'll always save you,' he said, his whisper earnest, sending my insides into an ooey gooey mess. 'We're past that childish shit now. We're a unit, a team. And to be a team, we need to stick together no matter what, the way we always should've done.'

'We were fourteen,' I pointed out.

'When our parents married, yeah, but not when we started hooking up with other people and ruining our happiness.'

'If I recall, it was *you* who started hooking up with other people…'

'Yes'—he nodded, a small smile playing on his lips that I wanted to bite off—'and I doubt you'll ever let me forget that.'

'Oh, one thousand percent!' I agreed enthusiastically, laughing when I was close to overdoing it. Ever since I met him, I thought Rock was beautiful in that way teenage boys are, but since we'd turned eighteen, he'd really come into himself—and his muscles. He was no longer a pinhead on a large body.

His fingers tangled with mine. 'It's time.'

'Why are you making it sound ominous as fuck like we're heading to our executions?'

'Because we might be.'

I swallowed loudly.

Well. Not like I could say anything to that.

'Arianna. Rock. I hope the two of you are excited for the time off school,' Dad said once the four of us were seated at the table in the formal dining room. 'And I hope you've both focused on your studies enough for exam time.'

'We're trying our best,' Rock said, digging into the starter the staff had just put in front of us. 'Studying whenever we have time.'

'Make the time,' Dad said gruffly. He lifted his wine and chugged the whole glass, then waited for a member of the staff to refill it. 'I've got a lot riding on you two.'

'Aside from my hand in marriage?' I murmured, and either Dad pretended he didn't hear me or he had nothing polite to say. Or maybe he was too absorbed by the food on his plate to be paying much attention to me. Dad did love his food.

'I'm sure they're doing their best,' Gigi said, touching my dad's arm, the way she always did when she was trying to calm him down or stop him from repeating something we'd spoken about at least ten times already. 'We've both raised wonderful children, Tony.'

He harrumphed, not deigning any of us with a verbal response, his dinner more important.

My dad had always had an appreciation for good food, but ever since he and Gigi started travelling constantly, he'd become even more of a food snob. His ever-growing waistline told anybody who met him exactly how much he loved his food.

The starters were eaten, then cleared away.

The mains were placed in front of us.

The wineglasses were refilled for maybe the third time in the evening.

And with every stage of the dinner, my heart was sinking further and further. At this rate, I'd have to scoop it up off the floor with my dessert spoon.

'Harrison left early last night I heard,' Dad said, and I wondered how much restraint he'd put on himself, not to mention it earlier. An hour had passed since dinner started, and I was impressed the man contained himself that long. 'I was expecting him to still be here when I returned.'

I waited for Rock's mum to pipe up, to stick up for me or to say literally anything at all, but she remained silent, swirling the wine in her glass, her eyes fixed on it as if it would answer for her.

Glad to know she had my back—not.

'He had to leave early,' I replied, flat, hoping he wouldn't pry too much. 'He left not long after Rock and Gigi got home.'

'Shame,' Dad said. 'And will we be seeing him again soon?'

It was now or never.

I took a deep breath, steeling myself for whatever came next. 'No, we won't be seeing him again anytime soon.'

'What's this about, Arianna?' Dad said gruffly.

It was now or never. 'Harrison and I have called off the engagement.'

Dad spluttered, spittle leaving his mouth as he tried to calm himself down, having choked on his wine at my announcement.

'Sorry?' he said, not sounding sorry in the slightest. 'You don't have the power to decide that, girl.'

'What, you mean I don't have the power to decide what I do with my life? Funny, but I think that's exactly what I *do* have. Power. Over my life. My body. And anything I want, actually!'

Okay, so maybe the speech would've come out better and landed a little better if I wasn't screaming like a banshee, but semantics.

I'd got my point across. *I think.*

'Arianna Hollowdale!' Dad growled. 'What has gotten into you?'

'What does that even mean?' I laughed, lifting my wineglass to my lips for a little more liquid courage. Couldn't ever have enough in such situations, after all. 'Why did you think I'd go along with your stupid plot anyway? Because I'm your daughter and you believe it's my duty? What the fuck, Dad? This isn't 1800.'

Okay, maybe I'd had more alcohol than I'd realised. My lips were a lot looser than intended, and the meek Arianna who usually let her dad walk all over her had left the building, letting in a much braver—read foolish—one in her place.

'Give me one good reason why you cannot marry Harrison Baker and I'll consider it.'

'One good reason?' I growled, my temperature rising. 'I can give you more than *one good reason.*'

'Enlighten me.' Dad's face was resolute, with barely any emotion flickering besides anger at me, and I knew he wouldn't believe me if I told him what Harrison attempted with me the night before. He'd tell me I had it wrong or that I was confused. Or some other male macho bullshit where the female wasn't heard because nobody ever believed the truth.

'Rock and I are sleeping together,' I blurted out. The pinch on my thigh from Rock was hard and I winced. That wasn't how that was meant to leave my lips, but once out, it couldn't be taken back. 'We're together.'

'You're what?' Dad roared, more spittle flying from his mouth and landing on the plate in front of him.

'Sleeping with—'

'Do not repeat that filth in my presence!'

'Filth?' I shouted, my tone the loudest it could be. Derision made me bold. 'What part of my sentence was filth, Dad? The part where I said we're sleeping together, or the part where I told you we're together?'

'Arianna Louise Hollowdale, will you stop fucking talking!'

'Oh sorry.' I sounded anything but. 'Do you have a problem with what I'm saying?'

'Arianna, dear,' Gigi piped up. 'Maybe you should refrain from saying more until your dad's calmed down a little. You know how he suffers with his blood pressure.'

Rock's hand was still placed firmly on my thigh, a calm and comforting boulder at my side, but he remained silent. Did that piss me off? I hadn't decided yet. He should want to speak up for me, right? For us?

But maybe he didn't want me to think he was fighting my battle for me.

'And I'm suffering under his oppression! Do you really want to lose me, Dad? Because this is where we're heading.' Tears filled my eyes and I tried to keep them at bay. 'I've done every-thing you ever wanted of me, Dad. I studied the subjects you wanted me to. I've accepted every new wife you've thrown at me. I've never refused you anything, not once. But this is *my* life you're messing with and I refuse to marry somebody who I barely even know. Especially somebody willing to touch a girl without permission.'

'Did Harrison?' Dad stuttered, looking angry still, but a guarded expression entered his eyes that made me think maybe it wasn't just me he was mad at.

'It shouldn't matter!' I screamed, frustrated that everything was blowing up in my face and nobody was coming to my rescue. 'What should matter is your daughter's happiness, not your fucking business dealings.'

'Get out of my house.' The words were clipped but certain.

'Sorry?' I scoffed, unsure I'd heard him correctly. I knew the conversation was going downhill, but I hadn't fully grasped just how far down it had gone.

'Get. Out. Of. My. House. Both of you!' Dad thundered, his face turning a dark purple that didn't look very healthy at all. Maybe we should call a doctor for him…

'Tony,' Gigi said, placating, touching the top of his arm. 'Maybe we should—'

'No.' Dad's furious eyes remained on me, not turning to acknowledge his wife. 'I want you both out of my sight and out of my home within the next ten minutes. I will not be held responsible for my actions if you're still here after that.'

Rock stood, still silent, and pulled me up, his hand having found mine. Without much choice, I stood too—it was either that or have my arm pulled out of its socket.

'Come on, Ari,' Rock murmured, tugging me harder.

Oh, he speaks!

I followed him out of the room, the severity of the situation not fully set in just yet. Rock whispered the moment the dining room door slammed shut behind us. 'Do you think we have time to grab some things?'

'He sounded pretty serious.'

'Where are we gonna go?' Rock asked and I shrugged.

'No idea just yet, but let's get outside before my dad decides to follow through on his threat.'

'Ari, your dad would never harm you. He isn't like that.'

'No, but who knows what deal he had with the Bakers. I might've really fucked up something big for him.'

'And he was willing to fuck up *your life* to get it,' Rock pointed out.

The truth was always a bitter pill to swallow.

age 18, march

Dɪᴅ I think my dad would kick us out?

No, no, I didn't.

Did I think it was a possibility? Well, yeah, sure, but I didn't think he'd actually *do* it.

Ty, I've got a huge favour to ask

Shoot!

The rents have kicked us out. Can we come crash?

Sure, princess. You on your way now?

Be with you in ten! I owe you big time.

You're not wrong.

'Okay!' I said, rubbing my hands on my thighs as I turned to face Rock. 'I've got a plan.'

'And…?'

'And we're going to go stay with Tyler at his flat in town.'

'We are?' Rock's eyes narrowed on mine, and I could see the

uncertainty shading his features. Even though I'd told him that there was nothing between Tyler and me, I wasn't sure if he'd believed me.

And there really wasn't anything between us—and if there ever was a small fondness growing, then it was gone now, and it had been gone for quite some time.

'We are. He's expecting us in ten.'

'Okay…'

'It's all going to work out, okay?' I opened the passenger door of my car and got in. 'Let's get out of here before my dad calls the police on us or something.'

'Do you really think he'd do that?' Rock laughed, getting in the car beside me, and I smiled, not quite ready to laugh at the situation just yet.

'Well, I didn't expect to be quickly throwing some stuff in a bag and getting out of dodge, so yeah, I suppose I do.' I shrugged.

'Touché.'

'Whatever happens,' I said once Rock had got comfortable behind the steering wheel, he'd needed to adjust the seat as he was a lot taller than me, 'we're in this together.'

'Of course.' He grabbed the wheel, pressing the car engine on before placing the car into drive. 'I wouldn't want it any other way.'

'Well, now that you mention it…' I trailed off, moving my gaze away from him to the window.

He stayed silent, and I couldn't stop the laughter from leaving my lips.

'I'm kidding, you oaf!'

'I love you, Ari,' he said, ignoring my joke. 'And no matter what, it's us until the end.'

'But…'

'No buts,' he said, shaking his head. 'Can we pause this conversation until I'm not focusing on the road?'

I laughed. 'Of course, but just so you know, I love you too.'

EPILOGUE
ROCK

age 18, april

IF YOU'D TOLD me at the start of the year that I would be moving into my own place with Arianna by my side as my girl, I wouldn't have believed you.

May even have punched you in the stomach for getting my hopes up.

But that was exactly what was about to happen.

Within twenty-four hours, the two of us would be in our own place, without disapproving parents. Plus, it meant Tyler could finally breathe in his own place.

When Ari had suggested asking to stay at Tyler's once our parents kicked us out, I wasn't all for the idea. After all, in my head, Tyler and Ari had spent the last year getting close and I didn't want to rub anything in anybody's face, but Ari told me I'd got it all wrong.

Tyler said the same when I spoke to him in private.

'Are you sure you don't mind having us here?' I asked, handing him a beer and taking a seat on the sofa next to him. 'Because we can go find somewhere else if you do.'

'Why would I mind?' he asked, taking the bottle and putting it to his lips.

'Because you and Ari had a thing…'

'I wouldn't describe it as a thing.'

'How would you describe it?'

He leaned forward, resting his elbows on his knees, a thoughtful expression covering his face. 'Have you spoken to princess about it?'

'No. I wanted to talk to you first.'

'I suggest talking to Ari about it, but honestly, there's nothing to worry about. We've spoken about it. We're all good.'

'I just don't want to put you out in your own place.'

'And you're not,' he affirmed. 'Swear it, mate. There's nothing to worry about.'

'Only if you're sure.'

'I am. I'd be honest if I wasn't.'

And that was that.

That was over four weeks ago now, and thank fuck Arianna had some inheritance clear so the two of us could afford to move without having to tuck our tails between our legs and ask our parents to take us back in.

'Are you ready for tomorrow?'

Ari was sitting cross-legged on the double mattress that was in the middle of the floor, surrounded by packing boxes all marked up and ready to go, and she'd never looked so beautiful. Her hair was up on her head in a messy bun, and her face was absent of any makeup. Cute pyjama shorts and a button-up blouse completed the look and for not the first time I realised how much of a lucky fucker I was.

'Everything's all packed,' she said, not looking up from the book in her hands. 'And Tyler's sorted a van to help us tomorrow, so we're all set.'

'Is Gray not coming to help?' I asked and she shook her head.

'Gray's got a lot going on at the moment. I didn't want to ask him for help with this.'

I nodded, understanding what she meant. 'You know he'd help. He's your best friend.'

'Yes, but he's also coming to terms with the fact he's going to be a dad later this year, so…' Ari shrugged, trailing off.

'Okay, yeah, guess we can let the guy off.'

'I'd say so.' She laughed, finally placing the bookmark on the page she'd stopped at, and gently closed the book before placing it down on the floor. 'Are you sure we're doing the right thing?'

'In what sense?'

'In not trying to sort shit out with our parents.' Her nose crinkled and I smiled at the emotion that ran through me. Nothing was better than knowing she was *mine* and mine only.

'I didn't think you gave a shit about your dad after the whole arranged marriage shit he tried to pull.'

'Well, yeah, that was a total dickhead thing to do, but at the end of the day, he's my dad, ya know? He did a shitty thing, but I don't want that to define him forever.'

'My mum's been texting me,' I admitted, sitting myself on the mattress next to her before removing my T-shirt. 'But I wanted to talk to you about it before I replied.'

'Do you want to talk to her?' she asked, turning her body to face me. 'Because if you do, then you should text her back. Arrange dinner or something.'

'Would you mind?' I asked, wanting to make sure I had her blessing before I did anything that could hurt her. That was the last thing I wanted to do, my mum's happiness be damned.

'Why would I? She's your mum, Rock. And we both know she's only taking such a hard line with us because my dad told her to.'

'I suppose…'

'Just message her, babe. You'll feel better once you do.' And as if that was all I needed, a weight lifted from my shoulders the moment the words left her lips. Ari knew what to say to me to calm me down, that was for sure.

'Have I told you lately that I love you?' I leaned forward to place a kiss on her temple, taking a subtle sniff of her vanilla scent before I moved back to look into her eyes.

'You may have mentioned it, yeah.' She smiled wide, a little laugh leaving her. Her hand tickled as she trailed it across my collarbone and up my neck, until she rested it upon my chin, pulling me closer so our faces were touching.

'I love you, Arianna,' I whispered, my nose grazing hers.

'I love you too,' she whispered in reply. 'Lots.'

'We're doing the right thing, aren't we?' It was the same question we'd asked each other a million times in the last month, but I needed to ask it again, just one more time. To be deathly sure. I moved back, watching her eyes as they became more certain with each second. The resolve was clear on my girl's face.

'We sure as fuck are. It just took us years to see it.'

'Nah.' I shook my head, shaking her words off. 'We both saw it years ago. We were just too chickenshit to do anything about it.'

'Yeah, that works too.'

We laughed softly, bringing our faces closer together again until we were an inch apart.

'We're going to be okay, aren't we, Rock?'

'Of course we are!' I said, maybe a little more enthusiastic than I felt. *Fake it until you make it.* 'Me and you, babe. Until the end.'

'Until the end.'

Epilogue

Remi

Everybody was always all smiles.

Laughing, joking, and just having a good time in general, with no care for anything other than their average day-to-day shit.

All while I watched from the outskirts, wishing I felt like that.

Could feel that happiness they all seemed to bathe in. Be carefree. Be able to joke around with my friends.

Fuck.

I'd have to *have* friends for that to happen. And that was the real kicker, wasn't it? I didn't have many people who gave a shit about me. Not anymore.

Maybe not even ever.

For a moment—a brief, fleeting, speck of dust in time—I thought Beth Jacobs was going to be that friend for me. The person I turned to in times of need. The person who was there for me no matter what.

But then everything happened and changed too quickly for me to keep up.

For my emotions to keep up. To accept.

I knocked on the plain red door in front of me, shuffling from side-to-side, agitated.

I wasn't even sure why I was there. *This is a mistake.*

Before I could turn away from the door, Tyler opened it, his dark brown hair falling into his eyes, and he brushed it away before looking down at me with concern playing across his features.

'Are you okay?' he asked, and I blinked up at him. Speechless for once.

Not even one bit, I wanted to say. But of course, I didn't do that. I *couldn't* do that. I blinked again.

'Of course,' I replied, trying to sound like his question wasn't necessary. *Of course I'm okay,* my tone implied, even though the sheer fact I was standing at his front door of all places made it clear I was the complete opposite of okay. 'Can I come in?'

'Er…' He looked behind him, shrugged, then turned back to me. 'Sure.'

Tyler opened the door wider and I took a deep breath before stepping inside.

Here goes nothing.

afterword

Thank you for reading Ari and Rock's story. I hope you've enjoyed it!
If you would like to join my newsletter to stay up to date with my upcoming projects, then scan the QR code below.

acknowledgements

Meg, thank you for everything that you do. Everything that you are.

Bills, as always, thank you for your wisdom and unwavering support—even when I'm just not feeling it.

Els, thank you for being there and for being an absolute babe. I appreciate you more than I say.

Fi, one day the penny will drop and something in your brain will click. I'll be there the moment it does.

Jess G, thanks for being on the receiving end of many of my frustrated and fed up voice notes, and for listening and never judging. I value you beyond.

Jess H, your friendship means a lot to me and even though we don't talk every day, or even every week, I know that you're there, regardless.

Thank you to my readers who have stuck with me throughout my journey.
And thank you to new readers, too.

about the author

Katie Lowrie is a twenty something year old Brit who loves to write the stories trapped in her mind.

A list in no particular order of her greatest loves:
- Henry VIII and the Tudor era
- Her baby cat, Cress
- Musicals
- Disney
- Cheese

She loves to stalk people online (in a good way) and understands if you do too.

instagram.com / katielowrieauthor

goodreads.com / katielowrieauthor

facebook.com / katielowrieauthor

bookbub.com / authors / katie-lowrie

also by katie lowrie

Rebels of Hollowdale High:

Haven at Hollowdale High

Hero of Hollowdale High

Heirs of Hollowdale High

Hated at Hollowdale High

Heartless at Hollowdale High

Hitched at Hollowdale High

Re-Imagined Series:

Key of Cunning (**Dark** Billionaire Romance)

The Sleep Eternal (**Dark** Mafia Romance)

Hawthorn Academy Series:

Disorder

Disease

Disturbed

Under the pen name K. Lowrie:

Model (mis)Behaviour

Acting Out